I0578291

IONA CARROLL

OTHER PEOPLE'S LIVES

SHORT STORIES

Silver Quill Publishing

Copyright © Iona Carroll 2019
www.ionacarroll.com

The right of Iona Carroll to be identified as author of this work has been asserted by her in accordance with the Copyright, Designs and Patents Act 1988. All rights reserved.

No reproduction, copy or transmission of this publication can be made without written permission. No paragraph of this publication may be reproduced, copied or transmitted save with the written permission of the publisher, or in accordance with the provisions of the Copyright Act 1956 (amended).No part of this publication may be produced or transmitted, in any form or by any means without the prior written consent of the author.

A Moment in Time was first published in *Carillon* March/April 2007. *The Visit* first Published 2006 as *The Irish Priest* in *Studio: A Journal of Christians Writing*. *The Snake* first published in 2007 as *The Irish Priest Revisited* in *Studio Journal*.

Published by Silver Quill Publishing 2019
www.silverquillpublishing.com

All characters and events in this publication are fictitious and any resemblance to real persons, living and dead is purely coincidental.

A CIP catalogue entry of this publication is available from the British Library.

Cover artwork copyright © Fiona Ruiz. Cover photograph of Balbriggan Lighthouse, Balbriggan, Co Dublin, Ireland copyright © Anne Walsh photocardsbyanne@gmail.com

ISBN: 978-1-912513-84-0

ACKNOWLEDGEMENTS

I am indebted to Oliver Eade for his advice and expertise in compiling this collection of short stories and also for taking the time to write the Foreword. Every writer needs an editor. I would like to thank Edith Critchley for her meticulous work in editing and proofreading this collection. To edit someone's draft is an act of generosity and I am grateful to everyone who has helped me.

Thanks to Anne Walsh for the cover photograph which inspired the short story, *The Perfect Model* and to Fiona Ruiz who created the cover artwork.

I would also like to thank Silver Quill Publishing for the opportunity to publish these stories.

There is a line in the poem, *A Toccata of Galuppi's*, written by the English poet, Robert Browning which has been with me all my life:

Some with lives that came to nothing, some with deeds as well undone

Inspired by these words, I have attempted in these stories to write about ordinary lives influenced by events and circumstances, sometimes beyond their control. It has been an enjoyable experience.

Dedicated to my granddaughter

Genevieve Waltl

CONTENTS

FOREWORD

I first came across Father Vic some fourteen years ago when, as a recently retired hospital doctor, I joined the Borders Writers Forum. We would often share our creative efforts, and one piece of writing, for me, truly stood out: a Father Vic story by Iona Carroll.

Since then I've read all the *Story of Oisin Kelly* novels, each one a gem. Indeed, *Homecoming* deserves a place among the great novels of all time that deal with the tragedy of war.

I was delighted to hear Iona Carroll has now published a collection of short stories, including seven concerning Father Vic, and I knew I would be in for a treat even before I started reading them. An established novelist, Iona handles the short story genre with a touch of genius. In *Other People's Lives*, she uses words to create snapshots of human experience. Although very different from each other, the stories are held together by a show of warmth and understanding. Pathos, humour and love are woven so compellingly into the author's writing that I'm sure most readers, like me, will not want to put the book down until *"...Miss Hatchett Met Sir Giles."*

Oliver Eade, novelist and playwright

A MOMENT IN TIME

When Mary O'Rourke ran past the hay shed on that hot summer's day, clutching a letter addressed to herself, she was eleven years of age. Ten minutes later, Mary O'Rourke was still eleven years of age, still held the letter, but she was no longer a child.

Later on, Mary would recall, if ever she could be persuaded to, that at that precise moment she had been happy as she ran around the shed. To receive a letter for Mary was a great event, she being only eleven and living on a farm. *We are pleased to inform you that you have won First Prize in the Junior Drawing Competition and enclosed is a Gift Voucher for £10.* Mary could not believe her eyes. She, Mary O'Rourke, had won a competition and was to receive a gift. It was all hers. And the first person she had to tell was her father.

Her father was a tall man. Spike, they called him, because he was indeed like a spike with his jet black hair grown longer than was the fashion at the time and a long black curly beard that covered half his face. When Mary looked up at him, she seemed so far down and he so far up, although she was getting taller, and now she could rest her head just above his belt. His blue eyes twinkled. He was sometimes cross, but it never lasted, and his eyes soon twinkled again. His bursts of anger held an unspoken pain, but Mary knew nothing of this. To her, he was a hero who solved all her problems, well, almost all. He was a certainty in her world for Mary lived in a world of adults; cushioned there, an only child, inhabiting this world with all its adult problems and adult fears, broken only by the farm animals, silent, non-judgemental companions.

It was a lonely childhood, but not an unhappy one. Mary loved her father and never knew her mother who had died when Mary was one year old, leaving a gap to be filled by her father's two unmarried sisters. No one ever spoke of Mary's mother — it was as though she had never existed, just lived to bring Mary into the world. Her departure was like some distant event that can only be described in an academic way, an event that was just dreamed about, and the loss perhaps too upsetting to recall. Mary had spoken about her mother only last year when she was ten because her best friend had asked Mary — 'Where is your mother?' Perhaps her friend had overheard an adult conversation in her own home and was curious. So Mary had thought about the question for a few moments and then she said, 'She's dead' — matter of fact as though the event had happened to someone else. And her friend had accepted this as children do, giving Mary's hand a little squeeze to say, 'I understand,' and had never enquired again. Only, Mary had thought about her mother last year and looked at her mother's photograph which she kept safely in her jewellery box. Mary had looked at the photograph a little more over the last year because to look at it made her feel happy.

So the first thought in Mary's head on that hot summer's day was to share her triumph with her father. She saw in her mind's eye, the twinkle of his blue eyes, how he would bend down, this huge, huge, man and be as proud of her as she was of herself.

'Well, Mary, you're a one,' she could hear him say. 'When did all this happen?' And he would read the letter again and again and smile so broadly, if she could ever see his smile hidden beneath that massive black curly beard.

So Mary O'Rourke had her letter in her hand and hope and pride in her heart as she sped to find this adored father. She trusted her father, trusted his judgement, he would not let her down. He held her in his arms when she felt little and afraid and lonely. Her joy would be his joy. It meant, at that moment, even more to Mary to see her father's pride than the winning of the competition.

She ran, her legs almost with a mind of their own, she ran, along the track past the hen run with the hens clucking aimlessly about, past the yard where the cattle were herded, along further to where the hay was kept for the winter in the big open shed, along and around the corner and then she stopped, stopped, and couldn't move, the letter still clutched in her hand, her feet all of a sudden refusing to function.

For Mary O'Rourke saw her father lying on the ground, half on his side, half on his back, his face sunk into the earth, not moving. Mary felt her life turn from movement to the slow painful motion of events that come, almost as if in a film, another person, another event, another moment. The life of Mary O'Rourke changed forever in that cruel split second. In that moment of fragility between life and death, Mary's childhood was gone. Gone, forever, it seemed, taken from her as casually as a leaf blown into the air, and disappearing somewhere into the blue sky.

She finally managed to move, to walk and then run to him. He was still breathing, she knew this, his eyes were open but something was wrong. She sank to the ground beside him. No tears. She didn't know what to do. She was only a child, just eleven years of age and so happy a moment ago, had been proud a moment ago, and now her world was changing as she fell to her knees to get closer to this dear man. She didn't know what he was saying. Mary put her ear close to his mouth, feeling the curly spiky beard prickly in her ear. If only she could hear, if only she could understand what he was trying to say.

In that grey moment between life and death, Mary waited to hear because somehow it must be important, that she had entered into this adult world prematurely which meant she must understand for some future date. She must understand so she could know why it was happening now. In that moment that changed everything for her, she was unaware of her familiar surroundings. All she could think of was this man, her dear father, lying there.

She gripped her father's hand. It no longer felt like his hand, it felt limp and cold as though the life had already gone from it, but Mary knew he was still there, still breathing. She heard him whisper a name. 'Jane'. Her mother's name – not Mary – but Jane. And she reeled back slightly, feeling a second of betrayal and almost anger. Then her father tried to move, tried to lift his head, but his strength was gone. He shuddered suddenly. Fell back onto the ground, his hand gripped Mary's ever so slightly for a moment, and then was still.

Mary O'Rourke sat back on her heels. Saw her crumpled letter — never, ever could she tell her father the news. She would never hear his voice again, nor see his smile. The blue eyes would not twinkle again. Ever.

And from Mary's soul came a cry of pain so intense that she wasn't ever able to recall it happening. On that hot summer's day, this was Mary's cry for all humanity's life and death struggle. In later life, Mary O'Rourke would wonder. But what, indeed, could she have done?

And Mary would begin as she grew older to understand a little of the nature of human suffering, begin to forgive herself for something not of her making, a reluctant witness to an event that changed her life. But that was a long time off, and another world away, and little Mary O'Rourke, aged eleven, a child no longer, could only hold her father in her arms, and weep.

A STRANGE TALE
A Father Vic Story

The scratching at the door became more insistent. No pause now. Scratch! Scratch! Scratch! Father Vic put down his book and listened. It was harder for him to hear these days and the hearing aid in his right ear didn't always work or that's what he blamed. He had learned to give all his attention to a sound by concentrating on his left ear with the result that he often looked quite comical in the way he inclined his head. Now he could really hear the scratching and it was getting louder.

When he opened the back door of the presbytery, he was surprised to find no one there. Instead a small cattle dog, tail wagging and eager to greet him, stood on the step. The dog was young – not much older than a pup - and without a collar. Father Vic could make out black pointed ears and black over the left eye. Father Vic noticed things. He liked dogs and dogs liked him too. Suddenly without warning, the dog fell onto its belly and cast its eyes downwards to rest its head onto the priest's foot.

'Well now... what do we have here?' asked Father Vic out aloud as the dog started to whimper. He lent down and stoked the animal's head and wondered what to do. The night was clear and frosty. Winter in the Outback could be chilly, especially at night, and Father Vic shivered slightly without his coat. He was about to close the door and let the dog fend for itself when he thought he saw a movement behind the oleander bushes. They grew on either side of the path and should have been cut back earlier in the year. Father Vic hesitated.

'Is anyone there?'

He thought that the sound was a cough, but he wasn't sure what he heard these days. He decided to investigate. The outside light didn't give much in the way of illumination and the street light was too far away to be of any use. As he walked somewhat hesitantly along the path, a spider's web wet with the night dew, brushed over his face. Vexed, he stopped to remove the sticky threads and then he thought he heard a man's voice:

'Are you the priest?' The voice seemed to come from the back of the oleander.

Father Vic squinted in the dim light to see that there was indeed a man there. He decided to confront the stranger, for who knows what poor soul was in need of his ministering care? The dog, on hearing the voice disappeared behind the largest of the oleander bushes.

'I am indeed,' answered Father Vic. 'Can I be of any help to ye? For it's a cold night to be sure... and not a night to be out too long.'

'Down, Bluey,' answered the voice.

There was no sound from the oleander bush and Father Vic suddenly felt anxious and didn't know why.

'If ye like to introduce yerself... I've already made the acquaintance of yer dog... I would be most obliged.'

At his words the oleander bush moved, and a man emerged from the shadows with the dog at his heels. Father Vic's first thought was that he was seeing a ghost. The man was a dark outline and the dim light from the street illuminated him eerily. A fine yellow sheen behind his head gave him a halo-like shape. His hat – the wide-brimmed style that the cattlemen preferred – was pulled down firmly over his eyes so that Father Vic was unable to discern much of a face underneath it. The man appeared to be wearing a black jacket and dark trousers. He was shorter than the priest and the priest was small compared to other men.

'Will ye come into the light so I can see ye a bit better? There's not much in the way of light coming from the street.'

The man didn't reply but stepped forward onto the path. Now Father Vic could see him a little better. He noticed that the man held a canvas bag in his left hand and he lent on a stick with his right hand.

'What would ye be wantin' with me?' asked the priest.

'I've heard that you're a man who listens to people,' was the answer.

Father Vic smiled.

'I've been known to hear a good many things in my line of work to be sure. Will ye come inside out of the cold... and bring yer dog with ye?'

The stranger hesitated. His dog had remained at his heels up to then, but it suddenly shot forward and stood looking up at Father Vic.

'Well now... ye have quite a dog here. 'Tis strange indeed... he seemed to understand my very words.' And Father Vic lent down once more to stroke the dog's head.

'Bluey knows,' replied the man. 'Yeah. I'll come in but won't trouble you too long. I'd be grateful for some warmth. I've walked from Sandy Creek.'

Sandy Creek was thirty kilometres away.

When the two men were seated in the priest's front room with the dog at the man's feet, Father Vic had a chance to study his unexpected guest. The priest judged the man to be in his late forties. There were furrows on the man's face, and his eyes were tired. This man had lived a hard life.

'I'm not a Catholic and never had any time for any church but there's something that happened to me over these past few days that's got me wondering. See this?'

From his canvas bag he took out a worn leather strap and handed it to Father Vic to hold. Father Vic studied it closer and then he realised that it wasn't a strap at all but a bridle. He frowned.

'I don't understand,' he said.

'Neither do I,' replied the man and lent back in the chair and closed his eyes.

'Are ye alright, man? Can I get ye a drink... a tea perhaps?' asked Father Vic, for he was shrewd enough not to offer anything stronger.

'No... I'm just tired. There's a story I want to tell and it's a true story... but who would believe me?'

The man paused as if he didn't know where to begin. Father Vic was silent. He fixed his gaze on the man's face instead. Father Vic had a way of putting people at their ease, so they spoke more and unburdened more with the speaking. He waited for the man to talk, as he knew he would. The clock above the mantelpiece rang out 'nine o'clock'.

'I've done some mean things in me life to both man and beast. Never known anything but the road and work when I could get it, and when I couldn't, I stole. Took from anyone and moved on. I've me dog and what a dog this one is! More human than most humans I reckon. Bluey knows things. Keeps me out of trouble. See that you've got hold of... that's a bridle. It belonged to a pony I stole. All I have

in the world is what you see in front of you... and Bluey.'
He paused.

'That here bridle has a story too... but first I'll just
warm my hands at your fire if ya don't mind, sir.' The man
rubbed his hands in front of the two-bar electric heater. He
sank back into the armchair and almost disappeared into
it, thought Father Vic. The priest was curious now.

'Well, sir,' the man continued, 'I was drinkin' with this
man a few months ago and we got to talkin'. This bloke
knew a doctor down Narrabri way and this here doc had a
daughter, about ten or eleven, and she was the apple of her
father's eye. Well, this here daughter was handicapped
somehow and couldn't walk very well it seems. But she
could ride a horse! Once she got onto a horse, she could go
like the wind. It was a miracle, people said, and this doc
spared no expense – the best saddle, the best pony – the
pony lived in clover because it made the daughter happy.
Well, this bloke says to me: "All's goin' fine till one day the
pony has a heart attack and drops down dead with the girl
on top of it. The girl's out of her mind with grief. She's
cryin' all the time, it seems." So I thought to meself,
"What's all this got to do with me?" He sighed and
repeated his question. Father Vic didn't say a word.

'Apparently, this here doc was beside himself with
worry too - for wasn't he a doctor and able to cure others –
but his own daughter refusing to do anything? Well, and
this is what this bloke in the bar says to me... the doc
decides the only way to get his daughter to see if she can
walk is to get her another pony, but it has to be the same
colour and size. No expense spared... the doc'll pay
anything. Now something lit up in me head when I heard
these words... it was like the proverbial light bulb turnin'

on. "What's this pony like?" I says to him and then I hear it an' I'm on fire with a thought. "I can get you a pony like that," I says, "We'll split the difference, straight down the middle." I knew he was interested... he was as mean as me. Takes one to know one, they say.' He leaned forward towards Father Vic and with a conspiratorial nod of his head, continued his story.

'I'm workin' for this here farmer, see? An' he's got a piebald pony, good natured little mare, stands about 14hh – she could be a twin by the bloke's description. So I says to this bloke, "I'll get you a pony – just tell me the doc's address and say nothing. No names. No questions asked. Agreed?" So we shake on it.' The man laughed.

'It all seemed so easy. I know the bush like the back of me hand. Lived in the bush all me life. A piece of cake to get a pony a hundred k's or so down the road.' He sighed. All this time he had sat in the chair without removing his hat but for some reason at that particular point in the story, he took the hat off to reveal a totally bald head. The heat from the electric fire had caused ripples of sweat to accumulate on the top of his head. Father Vic couldn't take his eyes off the man's cranium.

'Well,' the man said, 'all went well. I took the pony an' a saddle an' that bridle you're holdin', filled me bag with food from the kitchen and left in the dead of night. The dogs didn't even bark. We made good speed, too. We kept away from the main road and followed the river so as not to arouse suspicion, if you understand what I'm sayin'. Well, I'd arranged to meet this bloke from the pub on a certain day, at a certain time, at a certain place an' he'd have the money for me an' I'd give him the horse so no-one need know where it came from. Well, here was I, on top of the world, thinkin' to meself where I'd head for next with a wad of dollars in me pocket, when... an' I don't know what happened... but the pony stumbled and I can't remember for the life of me but the next thing this here dog is diggin' away in the soft sand... we came down at the side of the riverbank... the dog's diggin' away to free me foot. I'd caught me leg under the pony when she came down, see. She was finished... dead... an' me nearly dead too but for this here dog. I tell ya, I don't know where it came from but it saved my life. I had cracked the bone in me leg, see... that's why I need the stick now... but I managed to take the bridle, cut off the bit and wrap the strap tight around me leg.'

Father Vic could picture the scene, but he kept silent.

'To cut a long story short, sir... I was a changed man from that moment on. Somehow I gets the saddle off the pony... I don't want no evidence, see... and I hid it under some tussock grasses... got meself to the main road and hitched a lift... Bluey an' meself. I called him Bluey, you can see why, can't ya?' And both priest and man looked at the dog that was fast asleep in front of the fire. Father Vic could see the dark blue spots all over the dog's back.

'And this is where me story goes strange. They say truth is stranger than fiction... well, would you believe... it's the very same doctor who fixed me leg as the one I was goin' to screw with a stolen horse. He was a kind man too, and when he found out about me accident with the horse an' how it had dropped down dead under me, well, he went all quiet. What happened next is why I'm here to tell someone... I never spoke of it to a livin' soul... but they told me you are a man who listens to people.' He paused for it seemed the effort of recalling his story was tiring him. He had been talking for an hour and it was now pitch black outside.

'So this here doctor bloke asked me to do something for him. Would I go and see his daughter and tell her the story? I sure felt a heel but I agreed... guess I was feelin' guilty... well, his daughter was about ten or eleven sure enough and a beautiful little girl with long blonde hair and freckles all over her nose... it's no wonder the doc doted on her... there was just the two of them, see? I sat down beside her then and I couldn't stop talkin', told her everything... except that I'd stolen the horse... and Bluey just sits there listenin' to it all... now, this is the really weird bit...when I finished rattlin' on, Bluey goes over and starts lickin' the little girl's hand. You won't believe what happened next... as God is my witness... if there is a God, that is... this little girl who had hardly moved for a year, stands up, smiles and then she kneels down an' gives Bluey a God almighty hug. Then she turns to her father and says to him, "Do you think this man could get me another pony, Daddy?" Well, tell you, sir, I nearly wept right there and then in front of them! There's smiles all round and the doc is shakin' me hand, the tears streamin' down his cheeks. He's shakin' the hand of a no-good thief, the meanest man west of the Divide. An' I can tell you, sir, something happened to me at that moment for I've never stolen or cheated anyone since, and I've never wanted to either. You have to believe this, sir.'

And at that the man sunk back into the armchair and didn't say another word. He had been talking for nearly two hours.

'I've always believed in miracles,' answered Father Vic and he smiled gently. 'But then I'm Irish and a priest into the bargain... so what else can ye expect?'

Father Vic was thinking of the two robbers hanging at either side of the crucified Christ; one on the right and one on the left and of the one who was unrepentant only wishing to save his own skin and the other – remorseful, acknowledging what he was and in so doing redeeming himself at the final hour.

'I've an empty house,' Father Vic said to the man. 'There were three priests here when I first came... now there's only me... and a spare bed lying not used... you're welcome to stay the night if ye like.'

The man nodded.

'That's kind of you, sir,' he replied, 'Yes. I would be most grateful for your hospitality, sir. Thank you. I'm awful tired now. Be assured me and Bluey won't be any trouble. You've done more for me tonight than you'll ever know. Yeah... I'll stay.'

***

Father Vic woke to the enthusiastic call of the kookaburra perched on the telegraph line outside his bedroom window. Every morning the raucous sound heralded a new day and every morning Father Vic sent it a silent blessing, for the bird's cheerful sound was so different from the gentle twittering of the garden birds he remembered from Ireland. They woke him there, too, especially in the spring and he recalled how he used to lie in bed and try to identify each call but here, in this land so far away, the kookaburra laughed all year. Something would have been lost in Father Vic's world if he didn't hear the kookaburra in the early morning. He knelt beside his bed, the string of rosary beads threaded through his fingers, and prepared himself for his day. The peace of the early morning descended upon him and the repetitious prayers calmed his mind, and when he stood up to begin his day, a feeling of joy flooded him from his head to his toes. 'Praise be, dear Lord,' he murmured, and it was at that moment he remembered his guest.

He was looking forward to talking to the man and hearing more of the strange tale he had heard the night before. It was early – about six o'clock and Father Vic had an early Mass to say at eight. He planned to waken the man and explain his need for preparation beforehand but assure his guest of his hospitality. There was enough food for them both and the dog too, and Father Vic hoped the man would join him for breakfast after Mass — and maybe stay a little longer.

He knocked gently on the door to awaken the man but there was no response. He opened the door to a vacant room. He stared at the empty bed. *I don't even know his name*, he thought. Everything was neat and tidy, just as it had been. Father Vic wasn't sure if the bed had even been slept in.

'What's your name?' said the priest out aloud. 'I only know your dog... Bluey...'

Father Vic turned his head away from the bed. Behind his eyes he could feel silent tears, and he didn't know why.

A SUMMER'S DAY

It was hot again that day. For weeks Elspeth had woken every morning, early, to the promise of heat that sucked the life out of you. Elspeth didn't like the hot days much. It was even worse as she had to go to school and try to concentrate on what Mrs Jones was on about, and not be bored.

'I wonder when we're going to get rain,' her mother remarked to her father when Elspeth sat down to breakfast.

'Not today,' replied her father, putting down his newspaper and starting to shovel in his food like a giant JCB digger pulling up rocks.

'The creek's almost dried up at Sandy's place', chipped in Tom, renowned for his local knowledge.

'I'm not surprised,' his mother mused. 'It's getting serious.'

Serious or not, life on the farm must go on. The family had been through a lot this year — falling prices, rising costs and the death of Grandma at the beginning of the summer. Elspeth and her brother missed their grandmother. She had always been there for them. Their routine was suddenly and irrevocably altered and neither child liked it much. None of the adults seemed to be able to explain to the children, in any way that they could understand, why Grandma had to die. Elspeth missed her grandmother the most. Grandma and Elspeth had a special relationship, based on some obscure reason that neither of them could quite understand. They had both felt lonely sometimes in the midst of their family.

Their farm was an isolated one out on the plains, with the mountain range in the distance just a thin line on the horizon. The dark black mountains seemed to hold a promise that there was a world beyond, but so very, very far away. Elspeth had loved to sit beside her grandmother on the veranda and look over to the horizon. Here the two of them would sit; an old lady of eighty with a life behind her, and a young girl of eight with a life ahead, and both looked across that plain, one to wonder and one to know.

Not that Grandmother had travelled much, but she had crossed that mountain and found the other side. And that was enough for Elspeth. On that hot summer morning, Elspeth was thinking about her grandmother and how much she still missed her. So she decided to ask her mother once again about crossing the mountain range. She and Tom had only about ten minutes to get ready so in hindsight, as she spoke, she knew she'd picked the wrong time to bring up a sensitive subject - the reason for which she couldn't grasp.

'When do you think we could go to see Aunt May?' she asked with some trepidation because it always seemed to cause disagreement, but she thought she'd ask once again. Aunt May was Grandma's sister and lived the other side of the mountain. Elspeth had talked to Aunt May at her grandmother's funeral and thought that she was rather kind. Aunt May listened to her in much the same way as Grandma had. When Elspeth had asked her mother later about Aunt May, her mother had just said that it was too far to visit and that they couldn't leave the farm. But Elspeth thought that her mother looked a bit annoyed then.

Her father stood up without speaking. Her mother just kept tidying up the dishes. No one said anything or showed the slightest interest in Elspeth's question. It just hung there in the air like a balloon about to burst but in fact didn't burst, just fizzled out.

'You'd better get ready for school', said her mother, parrot-like, as she said the same thing every morning except on Sundays when she replaced 'school' with 'church'.

All day through the heat, Elspeth thought of that mountain range. It was visible from the schoolroom. She could look at it when she wanted to dream, which was frequent, especially today when it was so hard to concentrate. Hands were too sticky to hold pencils and the books felt warm to the touch. It was unbearable. Elspeth was so relieved to hear the bell at the end of the day, and she and Tom were free again.

It just seemed like any ordinary old day until the children arrived home. As they sped up the drive on their bikes, anxious to get inside to the cool kitchen for food and thirst-quenching lemonade or whatever they could find, a large white car stood in front of their house. 'Who's this?' Tom shouted, pedalling faster.

The two children burst into the kitchen like two over-excited puppies. What a sight greeted them! The room seemed to be alive with excitement. Their mother and father were both talking at once to the most beautiful person Elspeth had ever seen. This beautiful person was tall and thin with long blonde hair down to her shoulders and huge jangly earrings that swung back and forth as she was talking. Elspeth thought she just had to be younger than her parents. In truth, the elegant lady was only about thirty-five and her parents were about the same age. It was such a hot day that this vision of loveliness had on the minimum of clothing; a beautiful silk dress with bright orange flowers all over it and a pair of high-heeled roped sandals. She had bracelets on each wrist and her toenails were painted bright orange to match her dress. Elspeth stared in amazement.

'This is Aunt May's daughter, children. She's come all the way from London to see us. Come on and meet my children, Angela. This is Elspeth, the quiet one, and Tom, well, he makes up for it, don't you, Tommy?' said their mother. She put her arms around both children and propelled them in the direction of Angela.

Their mother seemed so proud; she was visibly puffed up. Elspeth gasped in disbelief. Not only was this person coming from beyond the mountain range, she was beyond the seas as well. It didn't seem to be real; it must be a dream. Nothing ever as exciting as this had happened to this family. The apparition was speaking to the children and she was speaking to them, not the way some adults spoke to children, as if they couldn't understand, but really talking to them.

'It's lovely to meet you both,' she was saying. 'I've brought you each a little present from London.' And from her huge bag she brought out two wrapped gifts and handed them to the children.

Tom started to open his present, eager to find out. His shyness gave way to astonishment when he discovered that this wonderful person had brought him a wooden model of the Tower Bridge. By pushing a little lever, the bridge opened smoothly. Tom kept pushing that lever up and down.

Now it was Elspeth's turn. She slowly opened her present, being careful not to rip the paper, and revealed a beautiful doll dressed in a pink satin dress with a satin hat to match. The doll stood erect on a stand and her shoes were made of pink leather and tied with pink satin bows. The doll had the most angelic face imaginable, and Elspeth could only stammer 'thank you', twice. Words had failed her, and she bit her lip, a habit she had when she was nervous or amongst strangers. She stroked the doll's satin dress and kept looking at Angela. And Angela sat beside her and she talked and talked about Grandma and the mountain range, and London, and all the most amazing places that were out there, away from the farm and the silent plains.

It was the most amazing afternoon. There was so much talking and so much laughter. Everyone seemed to want to talk at once. Elspeth had never seen her mother and father so animated. When Angela said:

'Looks like it's time to go, folks. It sure has been great meeting you all again, especially you two rascals', and she winked at Tom and Elspeth who both looked on with undisguised adoration. The whole family escorted Angela out to her car. Everyone was so elated and excited with the events of the day that they hadn't noticed the change in the air. The sky, which had been such an intense blue for months now, was now black with swirling dark clouds. Night had fallen but so had the clouds.

'There's a storm brewing,' announced their father, looking upwards.

'Thank goodness,' answered their mother. 'At last.'

'The end of the drought', laughed Angela. She bent down to Elspeth's height to say goodbye. Angela gave Elspeth a hug and a soft kiss on her cheek. Elspeth smelt perfume of a thousand flowers and felt a heart beating next to hers. A sudden charge of love rushed through every bone in her small body as Angela whispered into her ear:

'I'll see you in London one day, Elspeth, won't I? When you're all grown up...'

Through tears Elspeth could only nod but deep within her, so deep she thought that it came from something beyond herself; there was a sudden blinding flash of insight which

cried out for her alone to hear, and kept repeating and
repeating, over and over:
    'Yes, Yes, Yes'.

ALFIE
A Father Vic Story

As the years went by, and Father Vic aged, his waist measurement expanded as well. The kind and good-natured Father Vic had spent most of his life as a parish priest in the outback Queensland township of Jackman Creek. He was past retirement age and not as agile as he used to be. There had been talk of another younger priest to help him, but there didn't seem to be anyone about who wanted the job. Priests were getting rather thin on the ground these days so the powers that be seem to have decided that if Father Vic could manage, and he assured them he could, he would stay at Jackman Creek, at least for the foreseeable future. After all, he had been there for over forty years and part of the furniture, so to speak.

Getting about now wasn't easy. It often passed through his mind as to where his final resting place would be? He had long since given up hope that that would be in his native Ireland. Instead, he assumed that he would be laid to rest in the Catholic side of the cemetery at Jackman Creek, for the small township had been his home for so many years, and he counted the people who lived there his friends.

One of those friends was his housekeeper, Mrs Ryan. She looked after him in the way women do for men, and sometimes she fussed. Now Mrs Ryan, too, had grown old and wasn't able to cook and care for him as she had done for so many years. Instead a few kindly, slightly younger women from the parish had taken over the role of looking after Father Vic. His meals were cooked for him and the presbytery tidied by them on a rota basis, but Mrs Ryan still had the final say. She was rarely amused by Father Vic's antics and would have liked to see him safely tucked away somewhere in a retirement home, or wherever they sent the old priests these days, but Father Vic wasn't having any of it.

'Sure, Mrs Ryan, now in the name of God, what would I be doin' in one of those places?' he would say. 'There's still life in me old bones an' when the good Lord brings me home, it'll be when I'm ready to drop an' not before, praise be.'

For Father Vic was determined to carry on despite the increased measurements around his waist and the shortness of breath.

'Really he is the most stubborn of men, priest and all,' Mrs Ryan was heard to grumble. She would have liked to put the priest on a strict diet and see if that might help, but Father Vic had such a liking for the sweet foods of life she knew it would be a futile and thankless task. Instead, she rather sneakily reduced the portions at mealtimes and told the other women to do the same. Alas, kindly hearts liked to bake, and Father Vic was not one to say 'no' to a slab of chocolate cake or a cherry tart, his favourite. All to make up for the smaller portions, one might say.

'He really is difficult,' concluded Mrs Ryan. 'You shouldn't put temptation in his way.' But her scolding fell on deaf ears.

****

One summer evening, having eaten a particularly small portion of mashed potatoes, carrots and a meagre slice of cold beef covered in watery brown gravy left for him by Mrs Ryan, Father Vic fell asleep in his chair. Just before he nodded off, he ventured into the kitchen after

23

the good Mrs Ryan had cleared everything away and gone home. Much to his delight, he found the biscuit tin where he discovered an unopened packet of sweet Iced Vovos, his personal favourites. Father Vic had discovered these delicious biscuits soon after his arrival in Australia as a young man. These tasty biscuits, topped with two layers of pink fondant on either side of the strip of raspberry jam, and the whole delectable treat complete with a sprinkling of coconut became his preferred afternoon tea snack. Very quickly his parishioners discovered the young priest's sweet tooth and the liking for the humble Iced Vovo. In no time at all the news spread, and the biscuits took pride of place on the table whenever Father Vic paid a visit. So he set to work to eat as many as he could, and not call it the sin of gluttony, but rather this was to compensate for his meagre evening meal. Father Vic was very good at justifying his own behaviour and was certainly getting better at it as he aged. With this sensible thought in his mind and a smile on his lips, the good and kindly priest fell asleep.

He was woken about half an hour later to find the sun had gone down and the cicadas were hard at work to make as much noise as possible. He had brought the newly discovered Iced Vovos with him, now half a packet and minus the biscuit tin, and laid them on the coffee table next to his chair. He yawned and rubbed his eyes. Lately he had become rather absent minded and often fell asleep in his chair. Sometimes he would waken to find his glasses balanced on his nose and other times he would discover that his glasses were nowhere to be seen. Then he had to think where he had last put them and spend time looking for them only to discover, nine times out of ten, that they were beside his chair or had fallen off onto his lap. It was all rather irritating, and he grumbled that he spent more time than was necessary looking for the confounded things. This time he remembered that he had taken his glasses off and placed them in their case on the table next to the Iced Vovos because his head had felt heavy, and he knew he was going to nod off. When he popped his glasses onto his nose and stared at the table, the biscuits were gone.

'Sure, I must be losing me mind,' he said out aloud for there was no one to hear him, except the cicadas. 'To be sure, I don't think I ate the whole packet before I nodded off, now did I?'

And he shook his head. It really was a rather worrying situation for the old priest, this forgetfulness. He got to his feet rather shakily and grabbed hold of his stick. He needed a stick these days for walking had become rather difficult. It was then that he noticed the dog.

It was rather a large brown and black dog with four white paws and pointed black ears. Both Father Vic and the dog looked surprised to see each other and for a few moments, nothing happened. Then the dog gave a slight woof and took a few cautious steps towards the priest, and before Father Vic could say or do anything, thrust a long pink tongue onto the old priest's hand, and wagged his rather large tail which resembled an enormous feather duster. All the time the round black eyes gazed into Father Vic's watery blue eyes.

'Well, now, an' what would it be that ye are wantin'? For sure, ye are a grand lookin' fella, so ye are. Where in the name of the Holy Mother did ye come from?'

Father Vic did not expect an answer, but it was somehow a comfort to talk to the dog and not just mutter away to himself for once. He put his hand onto the dog's head and stroked him gently around the ears. The dog gave Father Vic's hand another swift lick of appreciation.

'What's your name then, boy?'

The dog wagged its tail with more vigour this time, woofed and stood upright on his hind legs so that Father Vic had to hold the two front paws in his hands, and the two of them stared into each other's eyes. Father Vic was short and fat so that the man and the dog eyeballed each other, and all the time the large dog kept wagging his bushy tail. It was then that Father Vic noticed something behind the dog. It was the packet of Iced Vovos, and that crumpled packet was minus the biscuits. All that remained on the floor were a few crumbs.

'Well, praise be, what have we here? To be sure, I don't think I ate all those biscuits, now did I? What do ye say to that?'

The dog licked the priest's hand once again.

'Have ye a likin' for the Iced Vovos as well, ye old rascal?' And Father Vic chuckled. It seemed the obvious solution in his mind for the empty packet. The dog replied with another lick and a whimper. Now Father Vic looked more closely at his unexpected visitor. It was clear to him that the large dog must be hungry for it looked decidedly emaciated, and the rib bones were visible. He wondered how it had managed to find its way to the veranda of the presbytery. Seeing the state the creature was in, Father Vic forgave the dog for eating the rest of the packet of biscuits. It seemed to him to be a charitable act and one that was worthy of his Christian calling. The dog seemed to understand the priest's magnanimous gesture for it gave the priest another lick on the hand and woofed once more.

Father Vic pondered what to do next. He had not seen the dog about Jackman Creek, and it was probably a stray. There was no collar around its neck and nothing to identify it. He speculated whether the dog had a name? It was all rather mysterious to say the least. The best course of action the old priest decided would be to inform his parishioners at Mass, and it might be a good thing to talk to the police sergeant as well. The local policeman was a friendly sort and knew everything about everyone in the district. Father Vic assumed that knowledge would apply to dogs as well, and with that thought in his head, he took hold of his stick and walked towards the front door, trying not to encourage the dog to follow. This ploy did not succeed, however. The dog trotted behind him and into the empty rooms. When the two of them got to the kitchen, Father Vic, now at a loss as to what to do, took the easy option. He filled a dish with cold water from the tap at the kitchen sink and found another slice of roast beef in the fridge. He cut the beef into pieces for the dog and helped himself to another slice. The large brown dog was grateful. It followed Father Vic into his bedroom that night and slept on the rug next to the old priest's bed.

****

The next few weeks were interesting ones for Father Vic and the dog. Although he made an announcement at Mass on Sunday and posted a notice in the newsagent's window, no one it appeared knew anything about a stray black and brown dog. Mrs Ryan was not impressed either.

'Whatever are you going to do about that animal?' she asked Father Vic just about every day.

'I'm working on it,' was the answer.

'Well, it can't stay here. Mangy looking thing, just look at it.'

The black eyes of the dog stared without blinking at Mrs Ryan. She found the animal quite intimidating. It was the size of the thing, and she wasn't very fond of dogs anyway. The presence of the dog in the presbytery was a new development, and she wasn't very happy with it. Father Vic, however, was growing increasingly attached to the dog. He was rather surprised about this and wondered whether this was some sort of divine test for him. Attachment to mortal things was not in keeping with his priestly calling after all. But this seemed to Father Vic to be a rather special dog, stray or not, and the dog was definitely attached to him. It followed him around all day and still slept on a rug at the end of the priest's bed. Father Vic had great conversations with the dog when they were alone and Mrs Ryan was not about. And, it had to be said, the dog was a great hit with the children. A little gang of young ones from the primary school arrived at the presbytery door after school just about every day, all wanting to take Alfie out for a walk.

'Why do ye call him Alfie? Is that his name?' asked Father Vic one day.

The children, three boys and two girls, all shook their heads.

'He just looks like an Alfie,' said one of the girls and she giggled.

Alfie wagged his tail and woofed.

'There, he knows his name, don't you, Alfie?'

'It certainly seems as if he does? Well, well now, isn't that the strangest thing?'

'You can call him Alfie too, if you like, Father.'

And so the large brown and black stray was named Alfie, and the dog seemed to like his name for he would come when his name was called and look pleased.

If Father Vic had lived anywhere else but Jackman Creek he would have had his driver's licence taken away from him years ago, but the police sergeant had thought it best just to let it be. The roads were as straight as a die and you could see for miles. Everyone knew the priest's old battered up Ford anyway. No harm was done, and more harm would have been done if the priest had not been able to drive for he would have found not getting out and about a cross too hard to bear, at least for the present. When Alfie was introduced to Father Vic's car, he showed no hesitation whatsoever. He jumped onto the front seat and sat down looking for all the world as if he was meant to be there. What could Father Vic do? A few weeks passed and the dog and Father Vic were seen together in the car; Alfie with his head out the window and Father Vic driving like the clappers. Both, it seemed, approved of the arrangement.

Dogs in Jackman Creek lived free. In this small community where everyone knew everyone else, dogs, and the occasional cat, were known by name as well, so it came as no surprise to anyone that Alfie soon became part of Jackman Creek and very much Father Vic's dog. Although it has to be said that Alfie was never very far from the good priest and vice versa. Alfie very quickly developed a routine which included a short walk to the butcher in the main street every late afternoon. Here to be rewarded with the occasional meaty treat. It helped that the butcher was a good friend of the priest and a stalwart member of the congregation. The dog became a stand-in for Father Vic whenever the priest was not there in person. This proved to be an altogether admirable and agreeable arrangement for Alfie, especially with the butcher.

The dog helped the old priest to get out walking as well, and although Father Vic's waistline remained much the same, his health improved with the exercise. Alfie seemed to understand that his new-found master was old. The two of them walked side by side at a gentle pace, and consequently the ritual was an altogether pleasant one for both man and dog. People stopped to talk. Father Vic, never at a loss for words even if those words were weather related, enjoyed the human connection. It helped ease the loneliness of the Irish priest so far from home, and that had to be a good thing.

He still had his moments of spiritual questioning as regards to the attachment that had developed between himself and the dog. He fretted, and sometimes he agonised about the situation. Should he find another home more suitable for Alfie? At these times, as if Alfie could read the mind of his benefactor, the black eyes of the large dog would gaze with such adoration into Father Vic's watery blue eyes that the question of rehoming became an academic one entirely. Alfie stayed.

One day about six months after the first appearance of Alfie at the presbytery, Father Vic, in his old Ford, with the dog beside him, sped along the road out of Jackman Creek. The old priest had taken to visiting a Protestant family, by the name of Earnshaw. The Earnshaws were farming folk and quite popular in the district. The family consisted of mother and father and three teenage sons. Both parents never tired of speaking about their offspring's achievements. The third and youngest son, a freckly-faced, ginger-haired lad of about ten adored animals and had plans to become a vet. So it was no surprise to anyone that Father Vic's new found dog companion, Alfie, and the boy became firm friends right from their very first meeting. Two of the boys had already left the district for the city, one to train as an accountant and the other to study law at the university. Whether it was the normalcy of the family's life or the generosity of Mrs Earnshaw whenever Father Vic paid a visit, no one could be sure about, but it was a fact that the old priest felt at home in their vast kitchen and told them so. Mrs Earnshaw was an amazing cook. Her pies were legend and her sponge cakes could not be surpassed. She had won First Prize at the Jackman Creek Agricultural Show for her sponge cakes for ten consecutive years. No wonder Father Vic liked to call on a regular basis.

There was also the matter of Father Vic's favourite Iced Vovo biscuits. When Father Vic happened to remark one day that these were his secret indulgence, and the biscuits would certainly be missed if he ever had cause to leave Australia, Mrs Earnshaw's eyes twinkled for she, too, loved Iced Vovos.

'Well, now, isn't that something?' said Father Vic somewhat surprised. 'And ye being such a great cook, Mrs Earnshaw, so ye are, and having a liking for these biscuits, just like me.'

Mrs Earnshaw puffed herself up. She was a stout woman with a large bosom and puffing up was easy. She knew she was a good cook, and the old priest was always so appreciative of her sweet treats.

'I like to take two Iced Vovos with my tea, you know,' the good woman replied. 'I reckon it's a break from my own cookin', you know. Or I'm just plain lazy!'

'Not at all, Mrs Earnshaw, not at all. I myself can eat half a packet of the biscuits in one sitting. I'm not for telling Mrs Ryan though,' he added, thinking of his housekeeper's penchant for trying to restrict his sweet tooth. Mrs Earnshaw was just the opposite, a fact that Father Vic rather liked.

'Well now,' said Mrs Earnshaw and she looked thoughtful. 'I'll have to see what I can do.'

The next time Father Vic paid a visit to the Earnshaws there was an unopened packet of Iced Vovos on the table for him along with the cup of tea and an apple tart.

'You're to take the biscuits with you, Vic, I insist.' She never called him Father. He rather liked that too.

'Well now, that's kind of ye. 'Tis the gift of a generous heart, to be sure.' And he tucked the packet into his jacket pocket.

****

That evening when Father Vic and Alfie had both been fed, the two of them adjourned to the veranda as was the nightly ritual. The large brown dog stretched out in front of the old priest and sighed. Then he positioned his giant head onto Father Vic's foot and closed his eyes. The priest smiled. They both knew that Alfie coming into Father Vic's life had made all the difference.

Father Vic opened the packet of Iced Vovos that Mrs Earnshaw had given him and took two of the biscuits. Alfie opened his eyes and sat up. All the time the big black eyes of the dog fixed onto the priest. Father Vic ate one of the biscuits, chewing it ever so carefully for his teeth were not

32

as strong as they used to be. Then he gave the other biscuit to Alfie.

For isn't it a fact of life that sharing and love inhabit the same world?

BLOOD ON THE SNOW

She was old now. Walking was difficult so that instead of walking, she shuffled, hanging on with arthritic fingers to her Zimmer frame. She muttered to herself as she tried to push the obstinate frame through the snow. The small wheels made movement difficult, and the last fall of snow had fallen onto icy ground so that the wheels stuck in ridges on the snow. She had to push and lift the frame at the same time, which meant that every few metres she stopped, panting and leaning onto the frame to catch her breath.

Age was to her a sad and sorrowful thing and her prayers, if she could call them that, were a pleading and repetitious cry for release from her poor, frail old body. But the lament for release was tempered with fear of what the next life would hold for her, unsure as she was of her record in this.

This winter's day as she pushed her way through the park, she felt something on her shoulder. She tried to turn but there was nothing there. A few more painful steps forward, and then she felt something hit her back. She felt the dull thud between her bony shoulder blades. Turning around, she thought she saw a glimpse of a small shape with a red woolly hat disappearing behind the old oak tree. Another small creature appeared to the other side of her:

'Quick, Jimmy, she's seen you.'

The old woman stood motionless, her face twisted in disapproval. It seemed to take her a few moments to fully comprehend what was happening. Two small boys pose no threat to an old lady. They had been busy playing, hurtling snowballs at each other and darting behind the oak tree as it was their "base", but the aim of six-year-old boys isn't as lethal as older boys and the snowballs rarely hit their target. The first one wasn't meant for the old lady, it was thrown by Jimmy to hit Brian, but it went in the wrong direction. The second projectile was thrown by Brian to hit Jimmy, but instead it landed on the old woman's back. Caught out, the two boys tried to hide.

The old woman understood nothing of this. All she saw at that moment was persecution and impertinence. Her Zimmer frame had a special place for a walking stick or umbrella; in her case it held her beloved hazel wood stick with its burr elm handle. It steadied her when she didn't have the frame; she could sweep up leaves with it, dig small holes with it. Now, she had another use for it. Out from its storage space it came, and she shook it threateningly at Brian and Jimmy.

'You cheeky young devils,' she cried.

The two little boys appeared together from behind the tree. For a moment they stared and then, sensing youthful dominance of the old, Jimmy answered defiantly:

'You're an old witch.'

This brought an attack of impotent fury from the old one. She shook the stick even more threateningly, and with her left hand tried to pull her frame and herself, towards her adversaries.

'I'll tell your mothers on you.'

Brian looked a little nervous – he knew his mother's wrath but Jimmy – who was the brighter of the two and looked after Brian if the two were ever in trouble, which was often, thought for a moment, and then answered with a triumphant wave of his hand:

'What's me mother's name then?'

This provoked more fury from the old woman, and she pushed her Zimmer frame and herself closer to the boys. This, however, had a different effect as the two of them suddenly seemed to synchronise and they began to circle her, running round and round, and getting closer as if to goad the stick into action. The whole surreal scene seemed to represent something from the African plains with the two young ones, lions, trying to bring down a feeble and dying wildebeest. And all about the park, people were walking, oblivious to the drama unfolding in much the same way as wild animals on a plain seem to ignore the cries of the victim.

Without uttering a word, the two boys started a new game which meant circling, and then running in closer to avoid the stick. All the while the stick kept being raised and dropped at unpredictable moments, the owner of the stick panting even more heavily each time it was lowered.

'Watch out, Brian,' cried Jimmy, suddenly alarmed at what he was about to witness because the stick came down dangerously close to Brian's head. Brian ducked out of the way, but he wasn't fast enough. The stick came down on his upturned hand. The knobbly bits caught Brian's young skin and two drops of blood fell like snowflakes onto the snow.

Victim and tormentors stopped, mesmerised, and all three stared at the drops of blood on the snow. Tears welled up in Brian's eyes, ready to pour forth.

'That'll teach you then,' the old woman exclaimed triumphantly, without a trace of remorse. Jimmy was in a rage of indignation. His friend had been injured by this ugly old woman. He reached down, and rolled a perfect round snowball, with such dexterity that it surprised him, and hurtled it at the perpetrator. The old woman turned, saw the snowball heading like a meteorite towards her, she raised her stick upwards, but this action caused the snowball to be deflected off the stick and it struck, like an avenging angel, onto the side of her head. She tottered forward, dropped her stick and clung precariously to her Zimmer frame. Blood dripped from the side of her head; there must have been small stones embedded in the snowball as Jimmy, in his haste, had grabbed snow from the path. The old woman was wounded, she fell to her knees; blood ran down her cheek and onto the snow.

At this, Jimmy and Brian, as if as one, bolted. Neither boy looked back nor did they stop running until they were in the safety of their own street, two blocks away.

****

Back at the park, a small group of three women had gathered around the victim.

'Are you alright, dear?' a woman was asking, and two others were helping the old one to her feet.

'She must have fallen on the ice.'

The old lady held onto her Zimmer frame and pointed to her stick, dropped when the snowball hit her.

'Have you far to go, love?' asked the third woman.

The old woman stared at her rescuers, and she was filled with a kind of silent fury at what she had become. Then somewhere deep in the recesses of her soul, she felt a glimmer of hope at the kindness of strangers for trying to help her, a frail, old lady, alone and afraid. She smiled thinly, and held out her hand to the three women, looked into their eyes and turned, continuing her journey, pushing and shuffling, the wound on the side of her face

37

still bleeding, leaving a trail of red droplets on the white snow.

He felt for the bottle in the pocket of his tweed jacket. His favourite tweed, the one with the tan leather elbow patches, now worn; the same jacket, tailored just for him from Savile Row – when style meant Style, and life was simpler.

The bottle was heavy. From another pocket he took out a small silver cup, slightly tarnished but the words still visible under the brown – *Duty with Honour* – and the regimental Coat of Arms. He smiled. The warm and mellow finest Malt slipped down his throat, effortlessly, perfection in the afterglow. Above him, Eros, the God of Love, swung his golden arrow. *Ah, Love*, the man thought. He took another gulp, more this time.

'I'm an old fool,' he said out loud.

On the steps below him, a boy and a girl giggled, holding each other; couldn't stop touching each other; their fingers entwined. The girl whispered something in the boy's ear. The boy lifted his head and laughed. The man could see them in profile from two steps above, their backs to him. *I want to say something to them*, the man thought. The London traffic stopped and started. The man became aware of the glow of the car headlights in the dark, the street lights, and the people mingling about, and he thought – *I want to speak to the boy and girl. Offer them a drink. Explain.*

But you don't talk to strangers in the half light of London when the thin sliver of the first quarter of the moon shines down.

I've kept this Malt a long time, he wanted to say. On the top of the Gillow's sideboard in the drawing room, behind the porcelain vase Uncle Frederick brought back from China. There, undisturbed, without dust. No dust allowed. No dust on this particular bottle of Malt, circa 1962. No dust anywhere.

I should have opened it when I found out, there and then. Drunk it down as fast as I could, with no thought of its taste, its smell, its vintage. Drunk, and to be so drunk with it, I would not have heard. I should have done something. But I am a coward, he thought, *and I was then. Until now. Until tonight, but I am drunk now.*

The boy and the girl began to look as if they were about to leave. The girl took hold of her handbag, holding it close to her, protectively. Don't go, said the man in his head. Stay with me and have a drink. I'm a rich man. I have all that I want except...?

The whisky warmed him. There was a chill in the air and the cars slowed. Above, the moon slid behind a cloud leaving a thin line of light in the sky, and far below Eros glowed. The girl and boy stood up fast. In one motion they leapt to their feet and kissed. A long lingering kiss beneath Eros. The man stood up too, slowly. He felt the pain in his knees. Slowly he placed the bottle and the cup back into the pocket of his tweed jacket. The moment for speaking had passed. All moments for speaking had passed.

'I'm leaving,' she had told him tonight, 'Finally, this time.' Words she had spoken over and over again to herself, but now, at last, she could say them.

I'm a coward, the man thought. *I should have done something.*

FATHER PAT COMES TO TOWN
A Father Vic Story

When Father Vic put down the phone he was smiling. Mrs Ryan, her duster flicking closely nearby – not too close, but close enough – stopped, and lowered the red, orange and blue feather duster just as Father Vic ended the call. Mrs Ryan, faithful housekeeper to Father Vic for nearly twenty years was not given to much in the way of humour. Life had been hard for poor Mrs Ryan and frivolity came rarely. So, seeing the smile on Father Vic's face, she frowned.

'Well now, Mrs Ryan,' and Father Vic's smile extended to show his slightly uneven front teeth, 'we are to have a surprise.'

Mrs Ryan's frown deepened. She was unsure of surprises and preferred certainties. She had Father Vic to look after and the presbytery to keep clean, that was a certainty. Mrs Ryan rarely smiled. Father Vic, on the other hand, was of cheerful disposition. So that, when he noticed that Mrs Ryan had lowered her duster, his blue eyes twinkled.

'We're to have a visitor, Mrs Ryan,' he said, 'and he's arriving next week.'

Mrs Ryan's mind immediately sprang into action. Visitors to stay were rare these days and meant more work to be done. Her frown deepened.

'That's a surprise, Father. A guest in the presbytery, and for how long, may I ask?'

Father Vic beamed:

'Well, ye know him, Mrs Ryan, and ye never can say how long he'll stay for isn't he just the most unpredictable man ye ever knew? It's Father Pat!'

At the mention of the name the frown lifted from Mrs Ryan's face as if by a magic wand, to be replaced by an ever so slight smile. Suddenly, her duster came alive again and swished back and forth over the mantelpiece and danced onto the framed print of the infant Jesus in His mother's arms. There was even a slight possibility that Mrs Ryan began to hum a tune under her breath as the duster did its work.

'Oh, Father... why, that's good news... I'll have to make him his favourite apple pie. He'd like that, wouldn't he? And what about that old armchair he likes... we'll have to bring it in from the veranda, won't we now? And I'll need to get fresh linen onto the spare bed...!'

And Mrs Ryan almost skipped her way around the dining room as the duster transformed itself into a conductor's baton. Father Vic's smile expanded. Preparations could now go ahead.

***

It was a scorcher of a day when Father Pat stepped off the train at Jackman's Creek. He had left Sydney five days earlier and travelled first to Brisbane, where he spent two nights with the Dominican Fathers. Then he caught the train west. He was pleased to see the rounded form of Father Vic waiting for him on the platform. Father Vic's skin had never turned brown under the Outback sun but was covered instead by countless freckles. He always wore his white Panama hat in the summer. The hat had seen better days, but Father Vic refused to part with it. This hat

42

was as much an identification of the priest as his rounded, freckled face, so Father Pat was quick to spot his friend.

'Ah, Vic,' he said extending his hand, 'how's it going with you?'

Father Vic smiled and his blue eyes, half-hidden under the white brim of his hat, took on their characteristic twinkle.

'Ah, Pat,' 'tis all the better I am for seein' ye again.' he replied. 'Sure, Mrs Ryan has been all of a flurry ever since she heard ye were paying us a visit. Ye'll be wantin' a cold beer and to get out of this heat, won't ye now?'

And the two men walked side by side along the platform.

Never was there such a contrast in physical appearances as there were between the two priests. Father Vic was short and round. As his years had increased so had his girth. Now the old priest was quite egg-shaped. Father Pat was as thin as the proverbial rake and a good ten inches taller than Father Vic. Side by side the two priests were a comical sight, especially when they were engaged in conversation. Both slowed down and weaved as they talked. In Jackman's Creek, it didn't matter. Walking this way in the city would have caused problems.

Their physical appearance was as dissimilar as their backgrounds, so it was something of a mystery how they had ever become friends. But friends they were and had been ever since their first meeting at an ecumenical conference in Brisbane ten years ago. They were drawn to each other as moths to a flame and the two of them, when they got together, never stopped talking.

Father Pat was lively, and he possessed a devilish sense of humour which bounced off Father Vic, so that their combined banter would entertain them for hours. Father Pat, a widower with a daughter and grandchildren too, had entered the priesthood later in life. Now aged fifty-six, he was something of an adventurer, having been a bookseller at one time and then a shearer's cook. Never daunted, he found work for two years on a building site and even spent time as a merchant seaman visiting Hong Kong, Singapore and Southampton. Throughout all his varied experiences he had remained a devout Catholic, so it was no surprise to anyone when he decided to become a priest and devote his remaining years to the service of others. Given Father Pat's experiences, for once the church did the most sensible thing. They appointed their priest to inner city Sydney – Redfern, in fact – and here in this urban environment amongst the prostitutes and the pimps; the drug addicts and the alcoholics; the down-and-outs and all manner of struggling humanity, Father Pat was in his element. It was five years after his ordination that he first met Father Vic.

Father Vic knew that Pat had seen much more of life than he had. Perhaps that was a contributing factor to the strong bond between them. And Father Pat, after all, was a lover of all things Irish, and hadn't he two sets of grandparents who came from Ireland? There was also the matter of belief. Father Pat's faith never wavered. Father Vic, on the other hand, sometimes found pinning all your hopes on something unseen, to be a complicated affair. There were occasions, Father Vic knew, that his position as parish priest was under question in his own heart. He greatly admired Pat's trouble-free mind concerning faith and assurance of an afterlife. But Father Vic, the Irish priest, kept his doubts to himself.

'Well, Pat,' he said to his friend when the two of them were sipping their cold beer on the veranda, away from the heat, and Mrs Ryan nowhere to be seen, 'What have ye been up to in the big smoke?'

'I wouldn't want to be the teller of tales, Vic. Jackman's Creek is a long way from Redfern,' his friend replied, somewhat obscurely, Father Vic thought.

'Sure, Pat, we don't see much here. There was a bit of sheep rustling the other day. They caught the three brothers red handed, but the magistrate let them off on condition they return the sheep. Well, everyone knows them. No doubt when the dust settles they'll be at it again, but that's Jackman's Creek, not Redfern, as ye say.'

Father Pat smiled.

'Well, Vic... maybe not so different after all,' he replied.

'How's that then? I wouldn't think they'd be much in the way of sheep stealing in Redfern! Your flock are a somewhat different lot to what we have here in Jackman's Creek,' and Father Vic grinned, enjoying the pun.

Father Pat poured himself another beer.

'Yes and no. There was something of a rustle the other day amongst the winos, and it had a bit to do with a sheep.'

'What do ye mean?' asked Father Vic, surprised. He wondered if Pat was winding him up. A sheep in Redfern?

'It all happened in Abdul's shop. From what I can gather, there was just Jacko and Jimmy, Abdul and the sheep.'

'Ye're havin' me on, Pat,' chuckled Father Vic, for he was now used to the wry Australian humour.

'Not at all. Just the four of them – the sheep being the unwilling victim. Seems both Jacko and Jimmy had been on a bender. Neither of them had eaten for a few days, and I guess the sight of the sheep was just too much for them.'

'Now come on, Pat... ye can't be tellin' me there was a sheep in a shop in the middle of Sydney... even ye can't make up that story! Ye'll be tellin' me that Abdul became a Catholic next!'

'Well, now... that would be too much to expect... though Abdul's a great bloke and a friend to all... even Jacko and Jimmy.'

Father Vic poured them both another cold beer.

'Well, Jacko and Jimmy got hold of the sheep while Abdul was in the back room tidying up. It was late and closing time. The pair of them unhooked their prize from the front window and almost got out the door with it. If Abdul hadn't come back into the shop sooner than they thought he would, they would have got away with it, but old Abdul caught them in the act: "You bad men – my doner kebab – you bad men!" and with that he grabbed the meat, wrestling with it as Jacko and Jimmy tried to pull pieces from it all the while. Sheep stealing they were! So Jackman's Creek and Redfern aren't that different now, are they?'

It was as if a light bulb had been switched on in Father Vic's head, and he suddenly saw it all, Jacko and Jimmy, city lights, an irate Abdul... and the sheep. He burst out laughing.

'No, Pat. Ye're right enough there, sure. Not much different after all!'

***

Ten days later Father Pat prepared to leave. Father Vic was sorry to see his friend go. His mind had been on the Redfern sheep ever since he heard the tale. He had worked out a way of weaving the story into one of his sermons, and he was feeling quite pleased with himself. Maybe Father Pat's tale would go round the Jackman Creek gossip circle and the three tearaway brothers might have second thoughts about sheep stealing if they were to hear about it.

The two priests and Mrs Ryan said their goodbyes on the veranda of the presbytery.

'I hope you'll come back soon when it's a bit cooler. You brighten up our lives, Father,' said Mrs Ryan and blushed slightly.

'I'm telling you, Mrs Ryan – my life wouldn't be the same if I didn't have my place in the country with you and Vic – you haven't seen the end of me, mark my words!' And he winked.

At that, Mrs Ryan's ever-present duster took control of her arm. With a deft, and quite an uncharacteristic movement, swished the bright feathers over Father Pat's shoulders.

'Just taking some of the Jackman Creek dust away from you, Father... till the next time!' she said.

HARRIET'S FRIDAY

At thirty-eight years of age, Harriet Riley had settled into the single life with a curious mixture of resignation and defiance dependent upon the mood she was in, and to whom she was talking.

She lived alone now since a particularly unsuitable man named John had moved out of her life. Five years on, she was used to her morning ritual, but this Friday she slept in and her whole day slipped back half an hour.

Harriet's morning was precision timed from waking to leaving for her work. Most days it was a success. But this Friday was different. In her frantic rush along the street that morning, she somehow managed to hook the left heel of her white patent leather shoe onto a loose paving slab. As she hobbled on her right foot towards the bus stop, holding the damaged other shoe in her left hand, her usual bus disappeared up the street. All this meant that poor Harriet was ten minutes late for work at the Bank, and not in the best of moods. When she settled herself at her computer, she slopped some of the contents of her early morning coffee over part of the keyboard. This necessitated a furtive disguise of her misdemeanour before the manager arrived. As fortune would have it, the manager, a woman of routine just like Harriet, was nowhere to be seen. Harriet breathed a sigh of relief. Not for long though. A few minutes later there was a cheerful Reggie Haldane beside her desk.

'Doing anything this weekend, Hattie?' He enquired in his usual affable way.

'Yes,' snapped Harriet, not looking at him. 'I've got a hot date!'

'Ah-ha!' grinned the easy-going Reggie. 'Anyone we know?'

'No', retorted Harriet as she tried to concentrate on a line of figures which, all of a sudden, seemed to be jumping around the screen like little black dots with minds of their own.

She was annoyed at herself for being so irritable with Reggie whom she rather liked, even though Reggie, two years her junior, always seemed to be promoted ahead of her at every turn.

'It's still a man's world,' Harriet would remark to her friends. Reggie, with his black curly hair and blue eyes that always seemed to twinkle with devilish humour, especially around the girls. Many, many times she had thought about Reggie, wondering what he was like naked, speculating what it would be like to make love to him. But then, of course, there was Reggie's wife, Eloise whom he adored, and rightly so, because Eloise was lovely. Well, everyone said so, and Harriet had to agree but with some reluctance, if the truth be known.

Harriet had enough moral character not to take another woman's man. Not like her friend, Miriam, who was madly in love with a married man and whose life consisted of furtive assignations and promises that were never kept. Miriam's life seemed to revolve around this character. Anyone could see that he had no intention of leaving his wife but was, according to Miriam, intending to – one day?

Harriet was determined not to fall into this trap and after all, she liked her single life. This was when she felt defiant. Reggie Haldane was a good person. Harriet knew that. He didn't pretend to be someone he wasn't. That's perhaps why everyone liked Reggie. Yes, Eloise was a lucky woman, if there was such a thing as luck, and if it came into the equation. Harriet wasn't too convinced about luck. She rather thought we make our own luck but that was her idea and not worth getting into an argument about. Reggie was cheerful, dependable, and just the sort of man that Harriet would have given up her single life for – but Reggie Haldane was not an option. Harriet doubted if anyone at the Bank ever guessed her thoughts on the subject of Reggie. *And no one ever will,* she thought grimly to herself.

The day proceeded in a more orderly fashion until finishing time when once more Reggie had something to say.

'Have a good time tonight, Hattie.' He winked that devilish blue eye and gave a slight chuckle. He always called her "Hattie". No one else did. 'If you and your date want to come over...?' Reggie continued with the same lopsided grin that made him so attractive to the girls. 'Eloise and I are entertaining tonight... just a few friends... you're more than welcome to join us.'

Harriet felt ashamed at her earlier outburst that morning. She wanted to scream, 'Reggie, there is no "hot" date, none whatsoever. I'm not doing anything this weekend. Nothing at all. Just to the supermarket and a walk in the park.' But she just smiled, and said:

'Thanks, Reggie and thank Eloise, but probably not.'

'That's fine, Hattie. Have fun.' And he was out the door.

****

When she arrived back at her little downstairs flat, Harriet felt lonely. It had been a different sort of day.

Times like this she would have liked to have someone to talk to. She prepared her food, watched the television, but she was quite wretched. At half past eight, Harriet reached a decision. She would go to Reggie's get-together, make some excuse about her date, but just go and escape from her downstairs flat, if only for a few hours. Reggie and Eloise lived not far in the next suburb – a fifteen-minute drive away. As she walked up the six steps to Reggie's front door with its neat bookmark conifers in white painted planters positioned at either side of it, Harriet felt a moment of panic. Should she have come, would it not be better to go away quietly before anyone noticed?

But there was Reggie at the door, puzzled but smiling broadly:

'Well, Hattie – good to see you. But where's your date?' looking around inquisitively.

'He couldn't make it,' replied Harriet, trying not to look into Reggie's eyes for fear that the lie might be written on her face.

'No matter,' said Reggie, taking her arm. 'There's someone I want you to meet.'

And he escorted her into his front room which was full of chattering folk.

'Ah, there you are, Toby.'

This stranger came towards them – Reggie in replica, Reggie's black hair, Reggie's twinkling blue eyes, Reggie's cheeky grin, but taller and browner.

'Hattie, I'd like you to meet my tearaway cousin, Toby Haldane. You've heard me talk about my Uncle Tom. Well, Toby's his son. Toby's just arrived back from New Zealand...'

Reggie winked.

'Think you two might just get on.' And then Reggie left them.

Toby Haldane held out his hand to Harriet. They stared at each other, both lost for words, and in that instant Harriet knew that her single life was over, and so was the Bank and her neat little downstairs flat. As strange as it seemed to her at that moment and on that never to be forgotten Friday, Harriet Riley, aged thirty-eight had finally found her man.

MAY THE SAINTS PRESERVE US ALL

They're hangin' my Ned tomorrow morn. Holy Mother, Mary and all the saints above, hear me, for sure I'd rather it were me at the end of that rope. I hope the police and the worst one of them all, that Constable Fitzpatrick, may they all rot in Hell for 'tis a great injustice that they are doin' to my Ned. It was trouble the night that Fitzpatrick came into our home to arrest Dan for horse stealing. Fitzpatrick's a liar and a drunkard. Anyone would tell ye that. He tried to kiss my daughter, Kate. Ned and the boys were only trying to protect their sister's honour, but no one would believe my Ned, an' it was Fitzpatrick's word them in authority believed. It 'tis a mother's love for sure, but isn't Ned my first-born son an' I love him with all the breath that is in me, an' I'll love him till I die? For didn't I bring him into the world an' hold him to my breast, an' him lookin' for all the world like my wild man Red, God rest his soul. Holy Mother of God, I didn't want to see this day. Them in authority say he's a bad 'un, one of the worst, an' a thief an' a murderer an' his is a life of crime an' the whole Kelly gang the same, includin' me, but I tell ye this, being poor and sufferin' for it, takes its toll on ye but my Ned loves me. Why, when Red drank himself to death, Ned signed his Pa's death certificate and him only eleven years of age. So I'm tellin' ye this, I love my boy with all me heart. God rest him when his time comes. Ned's only twenty-five but I'll tell him to die like a Kelly, so I will. We may be poor but we all love each other so dearly. When they put the rope round my boy's neck, he'll know that to be true, God rest him.

I've had a hard life, so I have. I used to watch the sailing ships, their white sails flappin' like sheets in the wind 'gainst the blue sky, away back in County Antrim, an' them ships all full of convicts bound for Botany Bay, an' when my parents and me brothers and sisters, sailed away too, across all that sea, an' we arrived in Port Phillip, what a journey it was, but us all thought we was leavin' me emerald green, blood stained Ireland for a better life. I've been a rebel all me life, an' I'm as wild as the horses I've tamed. Sure, I defied me father when I met an' married me husband, wild John 'Red' Kelly. Red was a convict too, he was, transported for stealin' pigs, they says, an' Red and me thought then that Australia was the promised land. But there's no promised land for the poor. 'Tis all the same the world over. If ye are poor, ye suffer. Maybe we'll get our reward in Heaven, an' here's to be hoped them that made us poor take another journey downwards, an' there is some justice, after all.

They put me in gaol for takin' a spade to that deceitful little bugger, Fitzpatrick when he came lookin' for Dan. Sure, I walloped him that night an' I'd do it again. Judge Barry sent me down; a year I spent in Beechwood Gaol, and then here to finish my sentence in Melbourne Gaol. The judge, he gave me three years of hard labour, as if I haven't had enough hard labour in me life, an' me just givin' birth two days afore, to my wee Alice. Puttin' a mother in gaol with a baby at her breast, what sort of man was he? An' that sneaky little bugger Fitzpatrick laughin' all the way. They tell me he stood drinks all round when he heard I'd got three years. To be sure, I'd wallop that little bugger again, harder with me spade, an' next time, it would kill him for what he did.

I told them, after Fitzpatrick, there will be murder now, and so there was. Sure, my Ned and Dan did wrong but when ye have the anger in ye, some things can't be stopped. An' there's the anger in their hearts, an' it won't go away. I have the anger in me too, an' a temper that would kill anyone that would hurt me family. An' now my Ned's to hang from the rope, an' there's nothin' I can do. I am weepin' in me soul for my poor boy, God rest him.

The police went lookin' for my boys to murder them, don't no one say any different. An' sure, my boys had guns and they used them an' they killed, I'm not sayin' they didn't. They robbed banks and dressed up like the troopers to do this, but I blame a lot of the trouble me boys got into on me mad brother, Jimmy Quinn, leadin' my boys astray he did. I'd have taken a spade to Jimmy if I could, even though he being me own brother an' all.

Well, when they told me that Ned had been arrested after the showdown at the Glenrowan Inn, didn't I weep like a babe at the news? An' after that, they told me he was to hang tomorrow morn, but I could see him afore. I hadn't seen my boy for two years, but my Ned was no longer me handsome boy. He just lay there in his bed for he could not walk. His face full of bruises an' the grimness was on his face, but those dark, hazel eyes were still the same, still sharp, sparkling, though there were lines around his eyes. I held him in me arms like I did when he was a child, an' sure, the tears ran down me face like the River Main back home in Ballymena, an' then I kissed him on his cheek for this was my son an' he didn't deserve to die like this.

I'll not sleep tonight for thinkin' of my boy and what's to happen in the mornin'. They say I should pray but prayin' won't do a bit of good this time for Ned will hang in the morn an' there's nothin' I can do to stop it happenin'. I feel as if a part of me will hang there with Ned, danglin' at the end of the rope as the life is taken from him. All I can pray for, if I have to pray, is that it is over quick like and he is at peace at last in the next world, for 'tis a fact of life that none of us Kellys or me own family, the Quinns have got much peace in this. Sure, it's been hard, lonely most times, an' they tried to break us, but we were doin' alright an' we will survive. Be brave, my dearest boy an' heed ye mammy's words at the end. May ye rest in peace, Ned Kelly. God bless ye.

Ellen Kelly, mother of the infamous Australian bushranger, Ned Kelly, was born in 1832 and died in 1923. She had twelve children, raising them mostly on her own. Hers was a tragic life and she is remembered as being a strong and defiant woman who would do anything for her family.

MISS HUNTLEY'S AWAKENING

At precisely 4.30 p.m. Miss Huntley called Oliver who wagged his tail and gave a slight bark. Miss Huntley took Oliver's lead from its place behind the door, hooked it onto his collar and the two of them headed for the outside world. Every day of their lives for the past five years Miss Huntley and Oliver had engaged in this activity for it had become as perfect a ritual as getting up in the morning or brushing your teeth. Miss Huntley called it their 'doggy walk', and it would have taken an Act of Parliament, or a major earthquake, to disrupt their daily routine.

Miss Huntley had rescued Oliver from the local dog's home when he was about six months old. She was fond of telling the story of how she and Oliver had found each other. Now, Oliver wasn't the best looking of dogs. In fact, Oliver was downright ugly. His parentage was obviously many and varied, he had an unsightly brown blotch over his right eye, his tail stuck out at a funny angle and he walked with a slight limp. He was a dirty off-white colour and to make matters worse, he had uneven black and brown patches along his back. To Miss Huntley when he first stared at her in the dog's home, he was the most beautiful creature she had ever seen and, without bothering with another dog, had bundled him into her car. As she looked at the poor, unfortunate animal sitting beside her, she decided on a name for it right then and there. That very week Miss Huntley had finished reading *Oliver Twist* for the third time, and the story was fresh in her mind. One glance at the unfortunate dog that had fallen on hard times, and was a victim of man's inhumanity, had convinced her immediately that he just had to be 'Oliver'. So Oliver, now the fortunate one, settled down to his cosseted existence of two square meals a day plus titbits, a bean bag downstairs, a bed upstairs in Miss Huntley's room with a canopy over it with 'Oliver' embroidered in red thread along the edge. It was a perfect working arrangement for dog and human.

Miss Huntley lived in a tiny cottage which she had renamed 'Shrangri-La' after another favourite book. For thirty-five years she had been a faithful employee of the County Council in whose service she had dedicated her life to the sorting and filing of complaints, mostly concerning refuse collection. In all those years she had never done one thing that could be called "exciting". In fact, Miss Huntley's life had consisted of getting up, going to work and coming home again, year in and year out. She had never experienced anything of what is called 'passion', had never travelled more than three hundred miles from where she had been born and had never really done anything with her life, except get through it. And now she was sixty-eight years of age, grey-haired and waiting with genteel acceptance for the grim reaper to come. Not that this last adventure presented any worry for Miss Huntley who felt her sins were so minor as to be ignored and she would be welcomed into Paradise by a loving Father who would thank her for all the contributions and hard work she had done for the church, in particular for the hours spent embroidering clerical vestments and all those altar cloths. Miss Huntley was as confident of her place in heaven as she was about the rising of the sun every morning.

If you had mentioned to her that she had never experienced life, she would have been very shocked indeed by your remark because Miss Huntley felt she had seen quite enough, thank you, and if she had never known a —man's love or hugged her child or seen the sun come up over the Himalayas, she didn't think she had missed out on much. In fact, she secretly felt she had been able to arrange things to suit herself and often thought how better off she was than her fellow men and women who were constantly getting into all manner of trouble with each other, their children, in laws — or the taxation department.

Into every life, however, there comes an occasional upheaval, and Miss Huntley's life, filled as it was with a certain element of complacency and superiority, was about to be disturbed.

Miss Huntley had few friends, and those she had ever made in her life tended to be in far worse situations than she herself. They would come to her to cry over their troubles. Flattered, Miss Huntley would lend a sympathetic ear and give lots and lots of reassurances. After years of hearing all these stories with variations on the same theme, she was more than convinced that hers was the better life, and relieved she only had Oliver to care for. She was thinking this very thought as she and the dog made their way around the block on their 'doggy walk'. It was a pleasant sunny day, and Miss Huntley was feeling very pleased with herself. She decided to walk past 'Mon Repos' to see if her friend Elaine was there.

If ever there was a misnomer for a house it was 'Mon Repos' because behind its doors on any day of the week was about as much drama as the outbreak of World War Three. Elaine Willis was twenty-five years younger than Miss Huntley and fitted quite nicely into the older woman's lame duck collection of friends in need. Elaine looked to Miss Huntley for advice, which she never followed, and sympathy for which she craved. Elaine's biggest problem was Ted, her husband of twenty years whom she detested with an animosity which made Miss Huntley grateful she had never married. The other people who were present occasionally at 'Mon Repos' were the Willis's two children, Derek, who had left home to join the Merchant Navy and Gillian, who attended a secretarial college in the city and only appeared home about once a fortnight. Miss Huntley had met Elaine out walking one afternoon and they had struck up a conversation. Since then, they saw each other nearly every day, as Elaine was forever popping in to see if Miss Huntley was all right or to have a session about Ted.

Miss Huntley and Oliver went around the back of 'Mon Repos'. Just then, a distracted Elaine came round the corner with a tin of red paint in her hand and nearly sent Miss Huntley sprawling.

'Oh, Miss Huntley, are you alright? I'm so, so sorry, here, let me help you.'

She took Miss Huntley's arm.

'It's alright, dear,' said Miss Huntley, adjusting her hat. 'What on earth are you doing?'

'I just have to paint the kitchen. I can't stand it one minute longer and if I wait for Ted to do anything, well, you know how long I'll be waiting. Come in and have a look and tell me what you think. I started it this morning and I've been on it all day. What time is it?'

Miss Huntley looked at her watch.

'A quarter to five.'

'Oh, it can't be! I have to get some more paint before the shops close.' She looked at Miss Huntley. 'You'd better come in, I suppose.'

'No, no, we won't bother you. We were just out walking...'

Elaine opened the back door and practically shoved Miss Huntley through it.

'Well, what do you think?'

Miss Huntley looked at the kitchen. Elaine's paint job left a lot to be desired. There seemed to be as much paint on the floor as on the walls and Miss Huntley didn't care much for all the red.

Instead she said, 'Oh, it's very nice, dear. You have been working hard.'

She looked at Elaine who, all of a sudden, started to cry.

'Oh, Elaine, dear, what's the matter?'

She put her arm around Elaine who sobbed louder.

'I can't stand it much more, Miss Huntley. I just have to do something.' She blew her nose. 'I'm sorry, I shouldn't be troubling you... but... it's Ted.'

Miss Huntley knew it would be.

Elaine continued: 'He won't give me any money. Most times, I can manage but he says we have to cut down on expenses.... it's alright for him, he never does without anything. What am I going to do?'

She looked at Miss Huntley helplessly.

'But, Elaine, he can't do that to you? Have you nothing at all?'

Elaine shook her head.

'Then you must take some of mine. You can pay me back when you can.'

She opened her purse and handed Elaine a crisp, new twenty-pound note. Elaine shook her head and started to protest, but Miss Huntley firmly placed the money into her hand and said,

'No, dear, I insist. You must take it. I don't want to hear any more about it. Now, we must be going, mustn't we, Oliver? We have to finish our walk and you have to finish your painting.'

She took a last look around the kitchen and moved towards back door followed by a grateful Elaine.

'Oh, Miss Huntley, you are so kind and good,' gushed Elaine. 'I'll pay you back as soon as I can. I promise.'

'Don't you worry about it, dear. Any time you can. Now, we must be off.'

Miss Huntley spent the rest of her walk thinking how sorry she was for poor Elaine to be married to such a brute who kept all the money for himself, and how happy she was that she had been able to help.

'What would the poor girl have done if I hadn't gone round when I did?' she said, thoughtfully, to Oliver.

A week later, Elaine was sitting in Miss Huntley's living room. The money drama wasn't mentioned, and Elaine seemed to be in a good mood. They were chatting about all manner of things when there was a knock at the door.

'Now, who on earth can that be?' said Miss Huntley as she went to her front door followed by Oliver.

It was Ted.

'Is Elaine there?'

'Oh, yes, Ted, come in.'

Ted came in and seemed to fill Miss Huntley's entire room. He was a big man. As he stood there looking at Elaine, Miss Huntley was a little frightened. She had always been timid when men were around. The sheer masculinity of Ted and the way he was looking at the things in her tiny room, made her nervous. Oliver, seeing another male, limped over and licked Ted's hand. Ted didn't seem to notice.

'Come here, Oliver,' fussed Miss Huntley, annoyed at Oliver's desertion, 'leave Ted alone.'

'Are you coming?' Ted said to Elaine.

The whole atmosphere was charged with such emotion that it was as if the room was about to explode and the ticking of the grandfather clock was the bomb about to go off. Elaine looked at Ted but didn't answer him.

'Ted, will you have some tea?' asked Miss Huntley, to break the silence.

'No,' answered Ted, shortly. 'Well?'

Elaine got up. 'I'll have to go,' she said to Miss Huntley apologetically.

That night Miss Huntley had difficulty sleeping. She kept seeing the look in Ted's eyes and Elaine's response. It was as though she had caught a glimpse of a human drama of which she had no understanding. Up to this point, she had only seen Elaine's side of the story. At times she had thought it must be a little exaggerated. Now she wasn't so sure. At about three o'clock in the morning, Miss Huntley felt such an intense hatred for Ted that she surprised herself. From that moment, he became her bitter enemy and she was determined to do everything in her power to prevent him destroying her friend. She had no idea on what course of action to take but she was sure she could do something to save Elaine. With this thought in mind, she finally dropped off to sleep.

The next morning, Miss Huntley and Oliver knocked on the front door of 'Mon Repos'. Much to her annoyance and surprise, it was Ted who answered the door. He looked at Miss Huntley without speaking.

'Oh... er... Ted, is Elaine there?'

Ted continued to stare at Miss Huntley. He didn't speak. In those few seconds she had a chance to examine him closely. He hadn't shaved, and she caught a whiff of some sort of alcohol on his breath. He was smoking a cigarette. His shirt was unbuttoned at the neck exposing a liberal amount of grey hairs on his chest. Miss Huntley felt trapped and didn't know what to say. She was filled with disgust as she looked at the man in front of her. Ted continued smoking his cigarette.

Finally, he spoke. 'No, she's not here. She's gone away.'

Miss Huntley felt a spasm of fear.

'Oh... when will she be back?'

At that, Ted didn't answer. Instead, much to Miss Huntley's amazement, he turned into the house and shut the door, leaving her standing there.

Miss Huntley's thoughts came all of a jumble. She was filled with impotent rage at the thought of Ted's treatment of her, and a dreadful fear that something might have happened to Elaine. *What if he's killed her?* She thought. *I wonder should I go to the police... but what would I say?* She was trembling by the time she reached the safety of 'Shangri-La.'

Now, Miss Huntley wasn't made from the stuff of heroes, so in the end she did nothing. Instead, for the next few afternoons on her 'doggy walks' she went past Elaine's house but carefully, on the other side, to avoid seeing Ted. There seemed to be no activity at 'Mon Repos' and Miss Huntley couldn't make out what was happening. It was beginning to cause paranoia in her as she spent the time imagining she was seeing Ted, scared in case she did. All her other thoughts were directed towards Elaine and concern for her safety.

This situation couldn't go on for much longer, and the whole thing erupted in a most unexpected manner a week to the day that Miss Huntley had spoken with Ted at his door. Once a year Miss Huntley took the bus into the nearest big town where she would visit her optician who checked her sight and her glasses. It was usually an occasion for much preparation but this time she was so preoccupied with Ted and Elaine that she nearly forgot the appointment and only thought of it the night before. Consequently, she was very relieved when the optician said everything was all right and he would see her next year. She had an hour before she caught the bus home in order to be on time for Oliver's 'doggy walk', so she decided to visit her favourite department store and have a cup of tea upstairs in the cafeteria.

She wandered around the various departments on the ground floor, and was about to take the lift up, when she happened to notice a woman at the perfume counter. The woman had blonde hair and was a little on the plump side. She had a rather low-cut blouse and a skirt that revealed a little too much for Miss Huntley's liking. The woman was trying on perfume and joking with the man beside her. The assistant was laughing too, and the three people seemed to be enjoying themselves. Finally, the man paid for the perfume and gave the woman a familiar pat on the bottom much to Miss Huntley's displeasure. He turned around, and the recognition of him sent Miss Huntley diving into the gloves and scarves on the bargain counter. He and the woman left the store. They didn't see Miss Huntley, whose heart at this stage had just seemed to explode inside her, because the man she recognised was Ted.

At first Miss Huntley didn't have any idea what to do with this unexpected bit of information. To have discovered another weakness in her enemy's character was something she would have to think long and hard about. Her fears about Ted now seemed justified because along with his parsimony in relation to Elaine, and his drinking problem, he had just added adultery to the list. Miss Huntley had no doubt in her mind that the woman, who was trying on the perfume with such obvious enjoyment, was Ted Willis's mistress. The very word seemed to conjure up the forbidden in her thoughts, and she was at a loss as to what to do. It was only when she was sitting in the bus on the way home that she thought of Elaine. It suddenly occurred to her that Ted had a reason for getting rid of his wife. Miss Huntley went cold with fear and knew she must do something, but what? She could hardly go to the police who would just humour her and try to put her off. If she went to Ted with this bit of information her own life might be in danger. She had no friends she could call on, as she didn't trust any of them to keep quiet. She could hardly tell Elaine's daughter, Gillian, when she came home at the weekend about her father. The girl would be upset and shocked, and Miss Huntley wouldn't want to have that on her conscience.

The next few days were agonising ones, as Miss Huntley struggled valiantly between a sense of duty and her own personal fear of the outcome should she do anything. It was now about three weeks since she had last seen Elaine and every day brought her no closer to the solution. Even her 'doggy walks' which used to give her so much pleasure turned into a kind of obligation and, although she kept a close watch on 'Mon Repos', she saw nothing. The house seemed unoccupied. She didn't know Elaine's neighbours. So she decided not to ask them in case she aroused any sort of suspicion. Her whole life seemed to have undergone a total upheaval since she had first got involved in the drama. Try as she might she was unable to put it out of her mind. She had most difficulty at night when she tossed and turned for hours, and only fell into a fitful sort of sleep early in the morning, when it was practically time to get up.

That Sunday morning, as Miss Huntley sat in her accustomed place in the church, she took a little more notice of the sermon than she did on most occasions. The minister took from the text of Luke 17:3 which said, 'If your brother sins, rebuke him and if he repents, forgive him.' Miss Huntley felt the words were directed at her and was so conscious of them that she felt everyone in the church must be looking at her to see her reaction. When the service ended, she hurried from the church without her usual pleasantries. Miss Huntley had received the solution to her problem. She now knew the only course of action she could take.

For the rest of the day she went over and over in her head the plan of attack. After another fitful night she woke early on Monday morning. She dressed quickly, had a light breakfast, put on her hat and coat, and was out of the house by half past nine. She caught the same bus she had caught a few weeks before and arrived in town just in time to have her mid-morning cup of tea in order to fortify herself for her ordeal. Over her tea, she rehearsed in her mind just what she would say to Ted and what he would say to her. She knew he had his own office machines and equipment shop in the High Street. Miss Huntley found it without any trouble and, taking a big breath, entered the shop.

She marched up to the front desk and asked to see Mr Willis. The assistant said he was upstairs in his office and just to go up those stairs there, pointing to some steps at the back of the shop. Miss Huntley did. The next floor was filled with computers and photocopying machines. She had to weave her way through them to the back of the room where there was a partition with 'Accounts' and 'Enquiries' written on the glass door. Miss Huntley opened the door and received her first shock. Seated at the desk in front of her was the woman who had been with Ted at the perfume counter. Miss Huntley gasped slightly. The woman looked up.

'Hello. May I help you?' she asked politely.

Miss Huntley hesitated and then replied, 'Yes... I want to see Mr Willis.'

'He's in his office at the moment. Who shall I say is calling?'

Just at that moment, Miss Huntley heard men's voices and saw Ted come out of the room on her right with another man. They were laughing and the other man said he would call back next week with the equipment. They shook hands and the man left by the glass door. Ted turned around and saw Miss Huntley standing there. He didn't smile.

'Miss Huntley?'

Miss Huntley took her courage in both hands. 'I want to see you.'

Ted stood back to let her into his room. 'Kate,' he said. 'Hold all calls, will you?'

Ted motioned to Miss Huntley to sit down. She remained standing. She felt she would be in less danger standing up. She quickly looked around the room to make sure she knew the quickest way out should Ted get violent. He continued to stare at Miss Huntley.

'Where's Elaine?' she blurted out.

This hadn't been part of her strategy, but she was feeling so agitated with the way Ted was looking at her, that it just came out. Ted flicked some ash off his cigarette into the glass ashtray on his desk.

'Miss Huntley,' he said at last, 'you have an uncommon ability to interfere in matters that don't concern you.'

Miss Huntley winced.

'What have you done with her?'

Ted continued to stare at Miss Huntley. Finally, a great sigh seemed to come out of him, and he said, 'My wife, Miss Huntley, is dead.'

Miss Huntley was so surprised at this bit of information that her mouth dropped open. Before she could think of her own personal safety, she retorted angrily, 'You've killed her!'

Ted got up from his chair and Miss Huntley backed towards the door.

'How much do you know, Miss Huntley?'

Miss Huntley grasped hold of her umbrella. 'Enough... enough to know you've murdered the poor girl.'

Then much to Miss Huntley's surprise, Ted laughed. But it wasn't the laugh of happiness but a broken sort of laugh. Miss Huntley was very frightened.

'Ah, Miss Huntley,' Ted said at last, and he sighed. 'Have you never loved anyone in your entire life?'

He looked at Miss Huntley who didn't like the way the conversation was going. She had come here to confront Ted, and now he was asking questions! She had no intention of talking about herself to this man so to change the subject she took a courageous step.

'We're talking about you not me. You've killed your wife so... so you can... run off with... her!'

Miss Huntley pointed her umbrella in the direction of the outer office. Ted didn't seem at all perturbed by this remark instead he just said mildly. 'Well, you do know a lot, don't you?'

Miss Huntley nodded.

'Well, now, I think it's about time that you heard the truth. Not that there's any reason why I should give it to you as you've done nothing but meddle.'

He emphasized the 'meddle'. 'But I suppose you served some purpose in Elaine's life. And for heaven's sake, sit down woman, I'm not going to hurt you.'

Miss Huntley sat.

'Did you really know my wife, Miss Huntley, or did you just feel sorry for her and try to save her from her wicked husband? Do you think you can answer that, Miss Huntley?'

They looked at each other. Ted continued:

'Do you know that Elaine and I had no married life for the past twelve years? Have you any idea what that means?'

Miss Huntley lowered her eyes.

'Do you know what it's like to see the woman you love, the mother of your children, destroy herself? And there's nothing you can do to prevent it happening. Face that one, Miss Huntley. Do you know what Elaine suffered from? Do you know where she died?'

Miss Huntley shook her head.

'Elaine died in a mental asylum. She was mentally ill, Miss Huntley. She was one of the statistics people don't like to talk about. Did you ever notice her change of moods, her obsession that I was trying to kill her, obviously, yes, or you wouldn't have come here today? They have drugs to keep them stabilized but it was getting to the point that I couldn't leave her by herself for too long as I never knew whether she would attempt to kill herself. Or run off, she did that a few times, you know. The police brought her back every time.'

He paused. Miss Huntley couldn't think of anything to say.

'She was always wanting to be mothered, to be a little girl again, and then when I wouldn't do it, she had to find someone else, and you fitted the bill nicely. Poor Miss Huntley, nothing is ever what it seems.'

Ted looked at Miss Huntley. He seemed to be deep in thought. Neither spoke for a few seconds.

Then Miss Huntley pointed somewhat hesitantly towards the outer door:

'What about... what about?'

'Kate? I love Kate. I don't think I could have got through it all without her. All I want now is to make a life for the two of us, and hopefully, give her back something of what she's given me.'

Miss Huntley looked at Ted. 'I'm so sorry... I had no idea.'

She suddenly felt very vulnerable.

'No, Miss Huntley, you didn't. You've never experienced anything like this, have you now?' He paused and stubbed out his cigarette in the glass ashtray. 'But we can't avoid life by ignoring it, you know. Things happen.'

As she lifted her head and looked right into Ted's eyes, which was an act of bravery on her part, Miss Huntley knew she would never be quite the same again. Something had got through to her that had never been able to before. This man had done that. She held out her hand to him, and he smiled.

That night, lying in her narrow bed, Miss Huntley wept. She wept for Ted, and for Elaine, but most of all she wept for herself and for the life she had led. Oliver snored gently in the corner.

NEVER STOPPED CARING

Ma name's Tommy Fair, only I'm no that fair, not with the things I've done but I come from a fair toon, Kelsae... well, that's oor way of sayin it but the Sassenachs say Kelso, and that's their way. I've been gaun a lang time. And now I'm hame.

'Ye'll end in the gutter, Tommy Fair'. That's what they said to me in Kelsae. Ay. They were richt too. I've been around the world since leavin my fair toon way back. Left when I was eighteen and many's the gutter I've been in since then. Been in bars and fights an seen the worst... seen a man die in the streets yince with a knife in his ribs. Had a woman in San Diego, she says to me, 'Look at your hand? You're always holding a glass. You're a drunk.'

I knocked her about a bit then. I'm not proud of that.

I mind in New Zealand, it wis outside the People's Palace in Wellington... I'd been on a bender for a week or more... this Salvation Army lassie she says to me, 'Jesus loves you,' that was Claire, ye ken. They wis good for a meal an' meant well, I guess. Anyways, Claire says to me an she wis holdin one of them tins, ye ken the ones ye put the dosh in, 'Jesus loves you.' She said it twice, I mind.

Well, I grabbed her tin an threw it against the wall. Made an awfie clatter an a few coppers fell out. I mind that. 'Jesus disnae love Tommy Fair,' I yelled. 'Naebody loves Tommy Fair.' Then I thought of Nellie, she loved me, leastways she said she did, way back when she and me yaised to meet at the Abbey. I was drinkin' even then... could doon pints faster than any of me mates. Proud of that, I wis. More fool me.

'I didnae want ye near ma dauchter, Fair,' says Nellie's father to me an he wis a muckle big man, wis in the Polis. I wis scared of him when I was sober but took him on yin night after I'd had a skin fou. I thought Nellie loved me then. She wis scared of her Da too, that's why we met at the Abbey and that's why I left Kelsae, well... I had to...they all said I'd end up in the gutter, nae good for naebody. I widnae hiv been good for Nellie. I would hiv ruined her life. No decent woman would hiv had me... there's always been women... but no one like Nellie.

I've been a hard man an' seen many things in ma life. Seen things since I left the Borders that's not fit for the tellin, but there's no a place on earth like the Borders an that's the truth of it. I'm gled I'm hame... had to come hame to die... like the elephants. Ye ken they go hame to die so they say. Well, I'm the same. Ay, the drink wis the end of me. They were all richt. The doc in Embra gave me six month. It wis like a special announcement ye get on Gala days. 'Mr Fair... how can I put this to you? I think it best you put your affairs in order. I'm sorry.'

Sorry. He wisnae sorry. The surgery wis full of folk waitin to see him an he wisnae for tellin them all to put their affairs in order.

Well, that's that, I thought. The end of Tommy Fair, born in Kelsae forty-two years ago... soon to depart frae Kelsae. I've no had a drop since the doacter telt me ma days are numbered an that wis three weeks ago. Get yersel back to Kelsae, I thought, to the Abbey, to Nellie. Where is she noo? A grandmother nae doot.

But the Abbey would be the same though. Been there since 1128, so it's not for movin. Ye wouldna think I know the date, but I ken everything about the Abbey cause that's where Nellie an me yaised to meet. We'd lowp over the railings an' go to our special place where the gravestones are set in the wall. Nae bather. It's a canny thing sittin here where me an' Nellie yaised to sit lookin around at this braw place even if it's a ruin... all thanks to the Earl of Hertford and Henry the Eighth... the English always wantin to destroy what wisnae theirs to destroy.

'You're good at History, Tommy,' Mr Anderson telt me. The only thing I wis good at. But I always had a head for dates. God knows where that came from? But I like bein at the Abbey an' lookin at the stonework. It's a grand settin too on the Tweed. I've been everywhere but never seen anything to match it. Ye think I'm daft sayin that... maybe it's cause of Nellie.

I found a stone carving once, in the wall, of two heads.

'Take a look at this,' I says to Nellie and held her hand. 'This is ours... oor special sign... Tommy an' Nellie.'

'You daft ape,' she said but she stroked the heads too. Together we stroked the heads.

I'll look for the heads in a wee while but just want to sit a bit an' think.

Ye ken... I yaised to think there wis nae point in it all. Ye wis born, suffered and ye died, but now sittin here where me an' Nellie yaised to sit, lookin' up... I wonder? Been thinkin' of this place... took them seventy-four years to build. Built stane by stane to the Glory of God. Men laboured here for God an they say God is love. All the work that love built now a ruin but ye ken, that's nae matter. Even if there wis nothin' here, just a car park or a Tesco, it wouldna matter at all because once love built something here an that's the most important thing. That's the point.

Nellie loved me but I wis afeard. Afeard of love. An' Nellie knew. Women ken these things.

Somethin's happenin' to me? Jesus, I'm shakin' all over. Hasnae been so bad this week. Christ. I'm scared. I cannae stop the shakin'. What's happenin' to me?

I'm burnin' up. The sweat's pourin' aff o me.

'Is there someone there?'

I thought I saw something. 'Is that ye, Nellie?'

'I'm on fire but I'm calm inside. God Almighty, I'm calm inside. What's happenin' to me? *Jesus loves you, Tommy Fair.* They telt me that way back then. Where are ye, Nellie? Are ye there?'

It was the woman who saw it first. She was unsure what it was, and so she stopped walking, leaning on her hazel stick for support. There was a shape behind a rock on a grassy patch at the edge of the track. Most days she and Archie walked along this way. A second or two later, she resumed walking, talking to her husband in a hushed voice, but Archie being slightly deaf now, didn't answer. He was already past the shape and away in his own world which he was more often than not these days.

'Archie', she called, louder this time.

'Whit is it noo?' He turned to face his wife and said. 'Wull ye no daunder on wumman, thare's a storm comin.'

And sure enough, the black clouds were gathering over St Abbs Head and the air had turned cooler.

'Leuk,ower yonder... next tae yon muckle stane...'

'Cannae seeocht!'

'Ir ye blinn, man? Oweryonder!'

Archie took a step backwards and now he could see what was there, almost hidden behind the rock. He shook his head.

'Oo shuid gaun on. Dinnae fash yersel, ye cannae dae ocht for it, Aggie.'

But the woman wasn't convinced. She leaned over the shape and prodded it.

'Oo maun dae summit... the puir wee burdie's bin hurtit.'

'Thrapple it, yons whit I wad dae for it.'

Upon hearing his words, Aggie looked up and shook her stick, ever so slightly, but enough.

'Ye'll daenae sic a thin, Archie MacDonald. The puir

critter. Can ye no see, it's bracken a weeng.'

And sure enough, that was what she had first noticed; thewhite shape of a feather lying next to the rock, and the small bird unable to move. Thinking of her husband's words, Aggie sighed. She was a kind woman. The sight of the injured bird, the gentle black eye looking ever so fearful, the yellow beak open and hissing its vulnerability to the dangers it faced. Aggie, uncertain of what to do, felt her own heart beat faster for she hated to see another creature in pain. All her life she had cared for the unfortunate and less able and, if sometimes, those she looked after appeared ungrateful, this compassionate woman would forgive them, and in no time, she would find another creature, human or animal, to nurture. The bird made a feeble attempt to stand up on its spindly black legs, but the effort was not enough and it sunk down again onto the grassy patch. Both Aggie and Archie could see the injury on the wing clearly now. Blood oozed from the damaged wing and some tiny red droplets had settled further down towards the small black triangle on the wing tip.

'It's a wee kittiwake... maun hiv bin skaithed someway whan the ithers flew awa,' Archie said.

It was the end of summer and the sea birds had left the high cliffs. With their going, the tourists and the bird watchers would disperse and calm would return to the St Abbs area. But come the spring the birds would return, to nest once again on the steep black cliffs, to lay their eggs, so precariously balanced upon the ledges, and the cliffs would once again resound to the screams and calls of guillemots, razorbills, kittiwakes and gulls as thousands of birds squabbled for nesting spaces. Then the tourists and walkers would return as well, and be amazed at the sight of so many different birds along the shore and the cliffs as the puffins, shags and the beautiful yellow and white gannets, swooping downwards, torpedo-like, into the sea, for St Abbs Head was a magic seabird city on the Berwickshire coast.

'Win awa noo Aggie. Thare's nowt oo can dae for the wee burdie. This yin wullnae be jynin it's neebors for the lang journey oot tae the sea.'

Their eyes met, and such a feeling of sadness passed between them at that moment. They had often talked about the migration of their sea birds from the cliffs of St Abbs. It was a fact, Aggie said, that the birds saw so much of the world, and it was also a fact that neither she nor Archie had ventured very far, albeit once across the border to Newcastle and a few times to Edinburgh. They had met each other at the Herring Queen Festival when Aggie was sixteen and Archie, who had grown up in Eyemouth, was seventeen. That had been the beginning of their life together. They were married a few years later at the Eyemouth Kirk. Archie had moved in with Aggie in St Abbs, for Aggie could not leave her poor father, bedridden most of the time with arthritis.

'Weel, aw the kittiwakes ir awa noo, cept this yin,' sighed Archie. 'Oo wull nae be seein thaim agane tul the spring, thaim aw feedin on the weeng an gantae furrin airts oo'll nivver see.'

'Ay I ken.'

Therewas an air of finality about the statement, the certainty of life's transience. They were both nearing the end of their lives together.

'Oo'd better leave the wee burdie noo. Leuk at the sky,

the wund's stertin tae blaw coorse... thare's stormy wather on the wey.'

A few drops of rain had already fallen, and the feathers of the injured bird were sprinkled with moisture. The rain droplets had caused some of the blood on the bird's broken wing to trickle downwards onto the white feather.

They were about to move away when the kittiwake suddenly moved. It thrust its tiny body upwards, trembling, and for a poignant brief second it stood on frail little legs.The tip of the broken wing, now dangling and helpless, lay on the soft earth. The bird then let out an almighty squawk.

'Leuk, Archie, the wee burdie's leevin. Whit a fechter this wee yin is. Gin I wes to tak it hame wi iz... mebbe I cuid mend it's weeng... I've clooted up a when o puir wee critters in ma time, hiv I no juist?'

'That ye hiv, Aggie. That ye hiv.'

'I cuid leuk efter it for the wunter... an in the spring...?'

'Ay. Whan its sibs cam hame...?'

'Oo cuid gie it a wee shot, div ye no think?'

'Haud ma stick for iz, Aggie.'

With a sudden movement Archie knelt over the kittiwake, cradling the bird ever so gently in his large fisherman's hands. He ran his index finger downwards from the head of the bird to the tip of its tail, and all the while the captive bird hissed and trembled. It tried with one last valiant effort to bite the fingers of Archie's hand. He murmured softly as if saying a prayer, and then in a flash, it was all over.

'Och, Archie...'

Gentle was that moment between life and death as

Archie laid the dead kittiwake next to the rock where they had first noticed it, and this time, he positioned the little bird so that the broken wing was on the ground and the good wing was visible.

'Ye cuid nae hiv saufed this yin, lass. It widnae hiv lested throu the nicht, whit wi the trashie rain an mebbie a tod oot leukin for its denner, the burd had nae hope.'

Archie took his stick from Aggie, and held her hand like they always did on their walks together, for both of them were less steady on their feet these days, and it was good to have each other.

'Pull yersel the gaither lass an haud yer wheesht! Oo'll mak oor wey hame for the tea. Oo dinnae want to be caucht in this haar, div oo noo?'

Aggie nodded. Her face, wet from the rain drops and the tears that ran down her cheeks, looked towards the mist covering the cliffs of St Abbs Head. There wasn't a seabird to be seen. She gave Archie's hand a familiar squeeze, and the old couple turned to walk back along the track that they had walked together for so many years; this same track where once Aggie had skipped as a child, and in all weathers. She often thought that she knew every blade of grass, every pebble along the way, for was it not so that her whole life had been contained within these few miles? She imagined the young kittiwake and how it might have been for it on its first journey away from the cliffs that she, too, called home. How wonderful it would be to be able to soar upwards to the sky, and turn and fly down to the endless sea below, then duck and dive and feed on the wing and find your way, by some miraculous compass, to foreign shores so far, far away from the cliffs of St Abbs.

Archie's hand was firm in hers. He was a good man.

Had always been a good man, and that was something after all.

'Ay, Archie,' she said to him when their cottage came into view, 'it wis for the best, ye ken. It wis a cannie thin thit ye did for yon wee burdie.'

And all Archie could do was to nod his head for he, too, had been thinking of the little dead kittiwake and his own life, and life's journey for all living things.

OVER A FLOWER
A Father Vic Story

When Father Vic entered the church, Mrs Jones was already arranging the flowers in front of the altar. He was surprised to see her there as she normally came in on Saturday, and this was Friday night.

Outside he could hear the cicadas, noisy and incessant. They filled the air with their monotone sound, and Father Vic disliked them. It was still hot outside, and the expected afternoon thunderstorm, due at three o'clock, had not arrived today. An image of soft rain and mist and the bogs of Connemara came into his head as Ireland did to him, without warning, and often on hot summer Queensland days. The church offered no respite from the heat either. No cool stone walls of home but wooden walls and an iron roof. *Even Jesus hanging from his cross above the altar looked to be sweltering today*, thought Father Vic, and then corrected his thought quickly.

'Ah, Mrs Jones. Is it yerself here, and on a Friday?' asked the priest.

Mrs Jones looked up. Between her fingers she held a pink and white gladiolus, long stemmed and sword like. Sword lilies, that's their Latin name. Mrs Jones knew everything about gladiolas. She had been absorbed in her task, lovingly taking each flower – pink, yellow, white and red, and grouping colours together in a line and was about to arrange them, one by one, in the two ornate copper vases positioned at either side of the church.

Mrs Jones was slightly annoyed at seeing the priest there. She enjoyed her flower arranging days and the chance to be by herself, away from everyone. Her four children were her pride but sometimes, well, we all need some time to ourselves, she rationalised, and now Father Vic will say something cheerful and I don't want to be cheerful. Not today. Not today of all days — even if I should be doing the flowers tomorrow. She frowned.

'It is, Father,' she replied, annoyed for no reason at his Irish-ness and feeling guilty somehow for that.

'They are looking grand, so they are,' said the priest and took hold of a red flower, larger than the others, caressing the stalk in an absent-minded way. Mrs Jones frowned again. *He'll break the stem*, she thought, *and that one's the best of the bunch.* She suddenly wanted to take hold of all the gladioli and keep them to herself. *They're mine. I grew them. In her flower garden at the back of the house, the sunniest position, next to the wooden fence but far enough away from the neighbour's dog.*

'I grew them myself. That one's my favourite...'

It had been difficult this year to get them to grow, too. The ground had been so dry when she planted the corms, but they've come on with the summer rains. Now she had two beds filled with the blooms and the church could have some.

If only Father Vic would stop running his fingers up and down the stem, she thought. Father Vic was older than Mrs Jones by twenty years or so. Sometimes he felt awkward around her and tried not to look too closely at her. It was easier that way, he reasoned.

'Can I have the flower back now, Father?'

She held out her hand, but Father Vic kept running his fingers up and down the green stalk and touching the red flowers ever so gently with his other hand. He had that faraway look about him. *Thinking of Ireland, Mrs Jones* thought. *He must miss it. Wonder he hasn't gone 'troppo' like some of us, what with the heat and the cyclones and the cane toads – must drive him crazy. It's a crazy place and no place for an Irishman so far from home.*

Still Father Vic held onto the gladioli and didn't seem to hear Mrs Jones at all.

Suddenly the red gladioli became the centre of things. The priest and Mrs Jones both wanted it. Or so it seemed.

'Ye know, Mrs Jones,' said Father Vic, 'I happened to be looking up the internet the other day and what do ye know? Gladiolas used to be used as tributes to the Roman Gladiators, now what do ye make of that?'

'I wouldn't be surprised,' answered Mrs Jones, somewhat taken aback. She didn't know that bit of information and wondered why Father Vic had been looking up 'Gladiolas'.

She looked down at all her other gladdies, as she called them. All lying in a neat row on the folding table she had borrowed from the vestry – pink and white, 'Mexicali Rose'; yellow 'Tesoro'; white 'Ice Cap', all beautiful, but not quite as beautiful as the red bloom that Father Vic held in his hand.

Mrs Jones tried again.

'That's a Mirella you're holding – the variety, you know – red. I love the red flowers. It's so very beautiful, isn't it, Father?' and she cupped her hand towards the flower, wanting to take hold of it and feel the sword shaped stem between her fingers.

Father Vic smiled. He had a kindly smile.

'Well, now – what a knowledge you have, Mrs Jones. We are fortunate indeed to be able to admire these beautiful blooms in the church, aren't we?'

The red petals appeared almost translucent against the priest's white fingers.

'That's my favourite you're holding.'

'And I can see why... beautiful... just beautiful.'

Now Mrs Jones was lost for words. She gathered up some of the yellow blooms, her least favourites and placed them in the vase. Why, the red Mirella that Father Vic was admiring so intently almost didn't make it to the church! It had been quite a debate whether to pick it or not. Rather leave it and let it keep blooming for a while amongst the others in her flower garden. But no, Mrs Jones had thought, and a quick snip with her garden scissors and the almost perfect Mirella lay amongst the other flowers.

Father Vic still held the flower.

'How's Tommy?' he asked.

Mrs Jones stopped what she was doing. She frowned. In her mind she saw her husband, Tommy. The two of them facing each other over her basket of freshly cut gladioli with the red Mirella on the top of the others, as befitted its beauty. She looked at Father Vic. He was such a kind man and he tried so hard. His sermons were always entertaining, and the children loved him. A lump rose in Mrs Jones's throat, and she felt the tears behind her eyes. She didn't want to cry in front of the priest. She didn't want him to think she was just an emotional woman. Her lips set hard.

'Tommy's just fine. He just told me... told me today. I had the basket full ready to come over tomorrow... well, Saturday's my day, isn't it? But it's all changed, Father, so I came today. Yes. Tommy's just fine... he told me today... he's been sleeping with that bitch, Katie Hennessey,' she paused. 'Now will you give me back my flower, Father?'

REMEMBERING PARIS

Laura stared at the envelope with its flowing writing neatly crossed out.

'There's a letter come for you. I've re-addressed it.' Her sister had rung her last week, and with some excitement in her voice, added, 'from Paris.'

The letter arrived at last. The house was quiet and no-one was about. Paris. She hadn't been there for ten years, and only once.

She had been twenty-three years of age, single and enjoying her life. That year for some reason she had announced to her family, 'I'm going to Paris this holiday.'

She remembered that her mother had looked surprised, horrified in fact. And her sister, twelve years her junior, annoyed. None of Laura's friends had any interest in Paris, preferring the sun and the package holidays that offered the hope of meeting Mr Right amongst the sand dunes or the bars. But Laura had always wanted to go to Paris ever since her art teacher had given her such inspiration all those years ago. She dreamed of walking along the Champs Elysées and sipping wine at an arty café on the Left Bank. So she had gone, travelling from Edinburgh by train, across the Channel, on a windy day, she recalled, and on to Paris where the travel agent had booked her into a small hotel off the Boulevard du Montparnasse.

Laura took the polished sycamore letter opener that she had bought at a craft fair years ago. She neatly slid the knife under and across to reveal the letter's contents. What was contained in the envelope gave her quite a jolt. There was a brief note in the same flowing handwriting...

'Hi Laura,' she read. 'Been clearing out and came across these. Thought you might like them. Regards, Angus.'

And Laura held six photographs in her hand. Six photographs of that memorable seven days of her life which she always thought were the most exciting days of her whole life. Six photographs, and there she was, the Laura of twenty-three, smiling, in front of the Arc de Triomphe, in the boat on the Seine; and Angus, his arm around her waist, both of them smiling broadly. The two of them looking as if they were madly in love, which they were, at least, Laura was, and at that thought, a big tear welled up in her eye and rolled down her cheek and would have fallen onto the photographs had she not wiped it away with her hand.

Now after all those years she could indulge herself and remember Angus. The first two days in Paris had been exhilarating. She walked and walked and loved being there. She was alone, but not afraid, for how could she be frightened in that most beautiful of cities where men and women kissed on the pavement and spring was in the air? The second day, she took a seat at one of the outside cafès that she had dreamed about and had managed in her faltering schoolgirl French to order 'la soupe de le jour' from a slightly supercilious waiter, but when she asked for the bill, that's when the trouble started.

The supercilious waiter had become arrogant because Laura's French failed her completely with the amount and the money. The waiter started to wave his hands around in an intimidating manner. His behaviour caused a mental block to occur in Laura's brain. Flustered, she wished that she was anywhere but sitting alone in a café in Paris. At the point of despair, she heard a voice and looked up to see a young man about her own age, blue eyes and a shock of red hair and a broad grin who asked in, wonder of wonders, a Scottish accent:

'Can I help?'

Laura gazed at her rescuer, and then at the waiter who had retreated to serve another customer, but he still retained his haughty expression:

'Oh, yes please,' Laura blurted. 'I can't seem to follow the money.'

Red hair leaned over, took one look at the amount, and beckoned the waiter to the table and said something to him. The waiter bowed slightly. Laura didn't understand a word. Then red hair took a note from his wallet and handed it to the waiter, who stuck his nose in the air, grabbed the money and quickly withdrew, the tray balancing precariously on two fingers and a thumb.

Red hair sat down and grinned.

'Don't let them get you down,' he said with a wink and a triumphant expression.

'Oh thank you,' replied Laura. She was uncertain what to do next and mumbled. 'How much do I owe you?'

To that red hair answered, 'A walk and to hear a Scottish voice again. My name's Angus, what's yours?'

'Laura,' Laura said, and at that moment, she looked into his blue eyes and fell in love. Ten minutes before, she had wished she could be anywhere but Paris. Now she didn't want to be anywhere else. And that's how Laura met Angus.

***

Laura laid the six photographs out on the kitchen table and recalled each one as if it were yesterday. Angus was witty and outrageous. She had laughed for the whole time she had been in Paris with him, or so it seemed to her now, remembering. He had a French mother and a Scottish father. His childhood had been spent in St Andrews with many trips to his mother's family in Rouen so that his French was perfect. He now lived in Paris, working as a design engineer for aircraft components. Laura didn't have a clue when he talked about his work, and he talked incessantly, but it didn't seem to matter, just being with him was enough.

There had been no consummation of their desires, although the sexual energy between them was there, leading to long and lingering kisses because this was Paris, and everyone seemed to be kissing. They had held each other closely, and when the time came for Laura to leave, it almost felt like death. Angus came to the Gare du Nord to say goodbye. They clung to each other as if to let go was to let go of life itself, but then they parted, and Laura never saw or heard from him again until today when this letter and these photographs arrived.

Edinburgh, when she returned seemed small and provincial and dull. She thought he would ring, but no phone call came. Then she thought he would write, and again, nothing came. After a while, Laura buried the memory deep and never spoke of Paris or France again. Nor could she be persuaded by anyone to return to Paris, and she never talked about what had happened there. That was ten years ago. Now she had Euan, dear dependable Euan, and two-year old Sophie who bounced around the house and made everyone laugh. But, every now and then, Angus was there in the back of her mind like a sore that would not be healed and would not go away.

Her mother died. Her sister remained in the family home. Of course, Angus would have sent the letter there. He wouldn't know that she had left, had married, didn't know anything about those ten years, but to write such a matter of fact letter and send those photographs, what could it mean?

Laura sighed, because the truth was stark and revealing. Angus hadn't loved her, not like she had loved him. For Angus, Laura had been a delightful diversion, a chance to recapture the Scottish part of his being, to parade her around the streets of Paris as something of a novelty, to take photographs of her, and to fill in a week.

Laura was lighting the fire when she heard Euan's car drive into the yard and heard Sophie cry out, 'Daddy,' and run to the father she adored.

From her pocket, Laura took the photos, the letter and the envelope, tore them into pieces and placed them onto the flames. The last image she saw as the red glow transformed them was Angus's smiling face with the shock of red hair disappearing before her eyes. *Ten years of memories gone in four seconds*, she thought with a philosophical shrug of her shoulders. *Now he's gone from me forever.*

'Thank you Angus,' she whispered to herself. 'Thank you for sending the photos back to me.'

She turned around to see Sophie dragging Euan by the hand to see Mummy, chattering away to them both, and Euan's smile a different smile from the boy she used to love.

THE COLLECTOR

Childless Ethel Prendergast collected dolls, dozens and dozens of them. She lined them up like soldiers on parade and arranged them in neat rows at the bay window, and when there wasn't any more room at the window, her husband Bert built shelves for her. And the dolls increased in number, so that after a few years, Ethel Prendergast moved some of the more fortunate, because these were the ones she loved the most, into the bedroom that she shared with her husband. Now these favourite dolls had chairs to sit on until another shelf was built. There didn't seem to be any ending to the number that Ethel collected. But the dolls in the bedroom were special ones. Here Ethel could say goodnight and good morning to them.

Ethel's bedroom that she shared with Bert looked as if a man had no reason to be there. The room was all tiny floral patterns of pink and green flowers on the walls. The bedcovers were pink and frilly to match. It was difficult to imagine that the sexual act had every occurred in this room. The fixed eyes of a dozen dolls would surely have killed off any passion. If that hadn't been enough to damper desire, surely all the frills and pink would have done the trick. To make matters even more uninspiring, it had to be said, that the thick white carpet on the floor and the heavy beige linen curtains with their peony roses design, pink and red of course, added nothing of interest to this perfectly tidy, but totally boring, marital bedroom.

Ethel and Bert hadn't started out like this. They had married early, she being just seventeen and he a mere twenty years of age and no one thought, given their youth, that the marriage would last any length of time, but they surprised everyone. Thirty-two years later, they were still together, even though Bert had given up saying much, and Ethel talked to her dolls more than she talked to her husband.

Ethel had always talked to dolls rather than people. Her very first doll was given to her on her third birthday by her grandmother. This doll wore a pink satin dress and little white leather shoes. Ethel called her Amy, and no one in the family could fathom from where she got the name. No one in the family was called Amy. Amy had deep blue eyes that opened and shut and a red mouth which resembled cheap lipstick. Ethel liked to feed Amy with a bottle, sticking the teat as far as she could into the doll's open mouth. When she tired of that she would try to comb Amy's hair with her very own hairbrush. One day, Ethel cut Amy's hair, and she cried when she was told that Amy would not be able to grow her hair again but would always look like that from now on, big chunks of hair missing from the back of the head for all time. Ethel wasn't quite so fond of Amy after that. A new doll was bought for her. This one she named 'Doll' and drew squiggly lines with a red pen along the doll's arms and legs.

One day when Ethel was about six years of age, she spied an abandoned doll behind a shrub in someone's garden. The sight of this doll, a rather unfortunate looking cloth specimen wearing a blue and white spotted cotton pinafore, was too much for the young Ethel. She broke free from her mother's hand, and before anyone quite knew what was happening, grabbed the doll and held it tight to her chest. Ethel held on. Her mother, embarrassed now as Ethel's tears and yells grew louder, tried to coax the crumpled-up doll away from a determined Ethel. Unable to persuade Ethel to part with the doll, mother and daughter beat a hasty retreat to their house, and the triumphant Ethel added another doll to her collection. This one she named Polly. Patched up and washed, Polly remained with Ethel to this day. Polly sat at the bay window between a talking doll who said, "Hello. Have a cup of tea," with a Japanese intonation, and a traditionally dressed Swedish doll named Anna.

When Ethel married Bert at the tender age of seventeen, the rescued doll, Polly, and Anna, the Swedish doll, came with her. At first, these two were the only dolls in the small apartment in which the young couple lived, for Ethel was certain that she would soon become a mother of daughters and that all of them could then talk to Polly and Anna. What fun they would have for they would be able to collect more and more dolls, and she would teach her daughters how to make clothes for them and put ribbons in their hair. How she longed to have a daughter to dress up and dolls to talk to. Ethel was a meticulous and clever needlewoman and loved sewing. It was just a matter of time, she thought, but as the years went by, and nothing happened, Ethel changed. Now Ethel looked at Bert with different eyes, and deep down blamed him for her childless state. And after a while, the subject of children was a subject that was never mentioned between them, and Ethel began to search for more and more dolls to bring home. She trawled the internet to buy dolls and searched for them at garage sales and secondhand shops. She rescued them, patched them up and dressed them in different clothes.

Some of Ethel's favourites were the dolls from different countries. Lined up on the window sill was an international brigade of celluloid, vinyl and plastic dolls, with one or two rag dolls that never sat upright like the others. All Ethel's dolls had been given different names and the international ones were named to fit their nationalities. An Indian doll, in a gold silk sari, called Anita; an Irish redhaired beauty named Colleen and a tiny Japanese doll, made of antique china with a white glazed head, were her most treasured. The Japanese doll was one of Ethel's particular favourites, "My little Geisha girl", she whispered into the doll's ear. She collected a brash American doll with a leather cowboy hat and high legged boots. This doll she separated from the rest and called her Calamity Jane after the film because she was sure that doll meant trouble. Calamity held a tiny rope in her hand, and who knows what she might do to the other dolls?

Once Ethel retrieved a china doll dressed in dirty white cotton pinafore from an antique shop, haggled with the owner and came away triumphant. This one was Heidi, and Heidi was the special one. Ethel had argued for a quarter of an hour to reduce the price. Poor Heidi looked damaged beyond repair when she got the doll home, but Ethel set to work. She repaired one shattered glass blue eye and carefully aligned the head. She decided that the doll looked Swiss. Something to do with the white pinafore reminded her of *The Sound ofMusic* and she made a dark blue long-sleeved dress to wear under the pinafore. The doll was Swiss now. Then she washed and ironed the doll's clothes and sat Heidi next to her Geisha girl so she could learn Japanese and Heidi could teach her friend German or French, Ethel wasn't sure which language Heidi could speak. The Swiss doll was old, at least seventy years; Ethel thought, and had to be looked after. The Geisha girl was kind and respect for her elders was part of her culture, so Ethel was sure the two of them would get on well.

Ethel had a younger sister, Jane, ten years her junior who turned out to be everything that Ethel would have liked to be. Jane didn't collect dolls like Ethel. She had a husband and four children, two boys and twin girls, two dogs, four cats, two guinea pigs and a budgerigar, and no time for dolls. On the rare occasions that she paid a visit to Ethel, Ethel locked her bedroom door. The special dolls stayed hidden. The less fortunate ones on the window sill and the shelf in the living room were guarded by Ethel in much the way a Rottweiler would protect its mistress's property. When Jane and the children visited, Bert disappeared to his shed in the back garden, and Ethel prepared tea for herself and Jane and lemonade for the children. Everyone was offered plain biscuits, and Ethel frowned if one of the children dropped the tiniest crumb on the carpet. The four children, for their part, squirmed on the uncomfortable sofa and wondered why their strange Aunt Ethel had so many dolls, and no children.

One day when Jane visited Ethel with the children and the dogs in tow, a strange event happened. All four children perched on the sofa and tried to be quiet so as not to annoy Aunt Ethel. Their mother had told them over and over again that they must behave themselves or they wouldn't be allowed to visit their aunt again. The children thought that might be a good idea, but when one of the boys mentioned this to their mother, the statement was met with a scolding. So the four of them were doing their best not to drop crumbs on the floor or argue amongst themselves or spill any lemonade on the sofa and trying their best to behave.

The conversation between their mother and their Aunt Ethel wasn't in the least bit of interest to the children. The four of them jostled for space on the upright sofa, whispered to one other, and giggled from time to time at the sight of so many dolls. After a quarter of an hour of sitting like this, one of the twins whispered to her mother that she needed to go to the bathroom. Lucy, now free, slid off the sofa and disappeared out of sight. Five minutes later, she was back, and she was holding a doll.

'What's that one's name, Aunt Ethel?'

'Which one, dear?'

'This one, with the blue dress and the white apron,' asked Lucy.

'She looks spooky,' said her brother, Peter.

'She's not,' answered Lucy. Before anyone could do anything, she clasped the Swiss doll, Heidi to her chest, and poked out her tongue.

'Spooky!'

'Creepy!'

'Stop it, you two. Behave yourselves. Give Aunt Ethel the doll, Lucy.'

'No.'

Lucy pouted and held the doll even more tightly. This was too much for the boys. They slid off the sofa and danced around their little sister, waving their arms in the air, and all the time emitting loud noises similar to the sounds they had seen in the films they watched on television between the cowboys and Indians. Now Lucy started to cry but she kept hold of the doll. A moment later one of the boys grabbed Heidi's leg and pulled it and the china leg came off in his hand. All noise ceased.

'You wicked, wicked boy, Peter. Look what you've done!'

Aunt Ethel's face was screwed up and angry. She looked as if she was about to cry too. She pulled Heidi from little Lucy's arms and rocked the doll in her arms, like a mother with a baby, cooing and whispering as she did so.

'Give me Heidi's leg, Peter. Poor, poor Heidi. She's in pain. You had no right to hurt her so much.'

Peter handed the doll's leg to his aunt without a word.

'I want you all to leave now. I must see to Heidi's leg. She's so old and frail. She might die. She's nearly seventy and the shock could kill her. All of you GO.'

Then Ethel, cradling the doll to her bosom and Heidi's leg in her right hand, marched out of the room. They heard the bang of her bedroom door. All four children and their mother stood in the living room not knowing quite what to do.

****

Jane was busy with hanging out the washing when she heard the phone ring.

'Damn', she said out aloud and ran towards the house. The voice on the end of the line sounded distraught.

'Is... is that you, Jane?' the voice said. It was Bert.

Jane caught her breath. She was surprised to hear the voice of her brother-in-law. He had never rung her before. Most times, he disappeared from sight when she was around. That was just Bert.

'I... I don't know what to do?'

Jane thought he might be crying but then dismissed the idea. Bert wouldn't do that.

'Whatever's the matter, Bert?'

'It's Ethel. She's gone away.'

'What do you mean, Bert? Gone away?'

Now she was certain he was in tears. She could hear him sniffing, and then he cleared his throat in an attempt to control his emotions.

'After you left the other day, Ethel locked herself in our bedroom and wouldn't come out. She took all the dolls from the windowsill and the shelf in the living room into the bedroom. I tried to coax her out, but she just kept saying over and over, "Go away. Go away". I brought her food and drink, but she wouldn't open the door. She... she stayed in the room for three days and nights... I had to sleep in the spare room... Jane, what was I to do? You know how she is with the dolls, don't you? We all do.'

Jane shivered despite the fact it was a warm sunny day. Something had happened to Ethel and no one had been there to help, just Bert. There was a pause and she heard Bert cough.

'I had to do something, Jane,' he continued. 'On the fourth day I rang the paramedics. They tried to get Ethel to come out of the room. Then they said they would have to call a doctor... and... the police.'

There was a silence, and Jane knew before Bert spoke next that something life changing had happened. It was the knowing before the knowing.

'They've taken her to the mental home, Jane. My poor Ethel. She didn't want to leave her dolls... so they let her keep Heidi. She wouldn't even say goodbye to me, just stared at me as if she wasn't sure who I was... a blank look it was.'

Bert didn't speak for a few moments. She heard him cough once again and then he spoke. He sounded a broken man.

'Jane,' he said. 'What do I do with all the dolls? I counted them. There's seventy-six. Seventy-seven if you count Heidi. They tell me it might be years before Ethel will be well enough to come home... if ever? What do I do with all her dolls? She so loved her dolls.'

THE INITIATION
A Father Vic Story

At Jackman Creek there was once a night like no other and, when the morning light brought relief to the weary souls, Stan Smith remarked to his mate, Billy Fogarty:

'That's some fella there – that young Paddy – we're lucky to have him!'

****

That young man was Father Vic from Ireland so far away, and all he could wonder at was the sights and smells of the Australian bush and be grateful to be of some use in the world at last. His arrival in the sleepy township of Jackman Creek could not have been less auspicious, for the summer sun was cruel that year and the ground brown and bare. Day after day, the sun rose in the sharp blue sky and the heat, intense and unforgiving, took the breath away. By midday both human and beast sought relief – the animals to stand huddled beneath the few gums that somehow managed to grow on the endless plain; the people in their houses with the overhead fans constantly whirring. The Irish priest, suffering sunburn and heat exhaustion, rose early every morning and longed for the soft rain of home. In later life he would recall that first summer as a kind of initiation that the good Lord had required of him. He hoped he had proved worthy. The people of Jackman Creek, however, remembered a different Father Vic that first year. To them, the heat of the summer was just a summer like so many they had lived through, before and since.

The priest's first friends at Jackman Creek happened to be Stan Smith and Billy Fogarty, brothers-in-law and farmers both. Kinship was a subject of great seriousness Father Vic discovered very soon after his arrival. He learned to be cautious before making any comparisons or observations for it was almost a certainty that he would be speaking of someone's cousin or uncle or childhood friend. Familial connections were written in stone and Father Vic, a city boy from Dublin, took his time to find out who was who. This way he avoided any embarrassment. It also soon became evident to the priest that the land moulded the people of Jackman Creek. Their vision spread out over that great silent plain, to the horizon beyond, and there it ended. The sparse landscape, which stretched as far as the eye could see, had made the Irish priest uneasy at first. His other world was filled with houses and streets and people packed tight, side by side. Sometimes when he drove for miles on straight roads, past farms and sheds and windmills, with only the occasional screeches from a flock of flamboyant parrots to break the silence, the young Father Vic would remember his other life and, at times, feel the sadness of the exile. To the people of Jackman Creek, Father Vic's Ireland, with its misty skies and soft rain and the seasons the wrong way round, was mystery indeed.

'Tell us about Ireland, Father,' the children said, but in truth, they weren't really bothered for that was the world beyond the horizon. Who would want to go past that line where the sky met the land? Even Stan and Billy, salt of the earth as they both were, sometimes grew weary when he talked too much of Ireland for wasn't it more important that the rains came and the price of wheat increased, and the Government after all, was always to blame?

In this way, Father Vic settled in but remained an outsider although his position as parish priest brought respect. *This is where the Lord means me to be*, thought Father Vic as he woke every morning to another pitiless, hot day.

****

One summer day something happened in Jackman Creek that changed all perceptions, and most important of all, it changed the young Irish priest forever. It was the hottest November day on record, and the night after that suffocating day, young Jimmy Fogarty, aged four, getting ready for bed, tugged his mother's skirt and pointed. She was busy at the kitchen sink. She didn't notice. Jimmy tugged once more. Finally she stopped and looked in the direction of the pointing finger.

At the precise moment that young Jimmy pointed, Father Vic happened to be driving along the road from 'nowhere to somewhere'; this was his name for the straight road that led to the horizon. He was late and it was dark. Already a canopy of stars shone through the black sky, and the priest could hear the curious sounds of the Australian bush. It was little wonder that Father Vic's mind was on cold beer and food. He had been away all day. The lights of Jackman Creek were already in view, twinkling as if brushed along the horizon by a magic wand. It was then that the priest saw the red glow. He slowed down and came to a stop outside a small weatherboard house. Now he could see the flames shooting into the night sky, the house aglow. He knew who lived there. Old Mrs Smith, Stan Smith's mother, grey now and weary but as tough as the land around. Here was a woman unbroken by life. She had the same courage as her fellow countrywomen; Mrs

Smith was a true Aussie battler. He had met the old woman a few times and liked her. Father Vic had no way of knowing whether she was in the house or not but the fire was vengeful. The house was crumbling in front of his eyes, and all he could do was watch, feeling powerless and afraid for the human life that was trapped in there. Here he was, a young man whose job it was to save. He heard voices and saw Mrs Fogarty and young Jimmy running towards him – Mrs Fogarty, Stan's sister,

'My mother... my mother...' she cried.

Father Vic took hold of Mrs Fogarty's arm. He thought she was going to rush into the house to try to save her mother.

Mrs Fogarty pushed him away. She started to run towards the burning house with Jimmy, crying, hanging onto his mother's hand, and the fire brigade nowhere to be seen. Father Vic he didn't know what to do. For a few minutes, all he could do was stare, like the others, just stare as the flames shot their arrows into the night sky, and the front veranda collapsed into a black red heap in front of them. Then he heard a voice. It sounded in his ear and he knew what to do.

'Get back,' he cried. 'Give me something for my head... a coat... anything.'

Mrs Fogarty heard the priest's voice and she unbuttoned her blouse. Her skin was white and her breasts hung inside her bra, but the priest did not notice. He covered his head with the black and white spotted blouse and ran towards the flames. The heat was so intense he could feel his skin prickling and his eyes watering. He ran over the wooden floor, the boards crumbled around him and his foot slipped into a hole. His breath came in gasps as he felt himself sinking. But something, someone, kept him going and he pulled his foot away from the smouldering hole, pushed through a door now open and starting to burn. He was in the kitchen. The flames leapt along the wall at the stove and the table in front was on fire. He had no idea where he was and what he was doing next, and no thoughts, no thoughts at all, only one... just keep going. The kitchen led into a sitting room and two bedrooms from there. The old lady had to be in there. This part of the house was not burning yet, but the heat was fierce. He thought that he might choke from the fumes. He managed to shout,

'Mrs Smith. Are you in there? Are you there...?'

Father Vic had strong shoulders. He had been a front row forward when he played rugby at the seminary in Ireland and now his strength was supernatural. He pushed hard at the door to the first bedroom, but the old lady was nowhere to be seen. He ran to the next room. The door was slightly open. Then he saw her. Old Mrs Smith was asleep with her hands tucked under her chin and her body twisted, S-shaped under the thin covers. The smoke was already in the room, and Father Vic's eyes, watering from the heat of the fire could just make out the thin shape in front of him.

'Mrs Smith,' he cried, 'wake up....!'

But she didn't stir. He cried out again and shook her – his hand on her thin shoulder – but still she didn't wake.

'Oh God! Please wake up... please!'

All manner of thoughts now rushed into the priest's head. He was aware of the gravity of the situation. The only way out had to be through the window because the fire had already taken hold behind him. He shook the old lady again and again. At last she moved, opened her eyes and looked around the room.

'What is it? Is that you, Stan?' For in the smoke-filled room she thought it was her son bending over her.

'Take hold of me... we'll get ye safe... 'tis a fire raging behind ye and no way out for ye but through the window yonder.'

He scooped old Mrs Smith into his arms, covers and all. She was as light as a feather for the young priest and no problem at all for him to hold. He climbed through the open window to the world outside.

He held old Mrs Smith tight in his arms till she moved and started to speak. Then the two of them stood side by side, the priest's arm around the old lady's shoulders. They stood together, and watched as her home and her life there, disappeared.

****

A small group formed a protective circle around Mrs Fogarty and her Jimmy for the fire was out now thanks to the volunteer firemen who had arrived in time after all. Old Mrs Smith, that hardy soul, was safe.

'Father Vic saved my mother,' sobbed Mrs Fogarty.

Stan, the tears running from his eyes, said,

'He's a hero, a bloody great hero.'

The good people of Jackman Creek knew that a rather special young man had come from Ireland so far away, beyond the horizon. They all agreed that this young man, a Catholic priest, had made his home amongst them for a reason, and he was a stranger no more.

The neighbours in the street in which he lived could tell the time by Dennis MacPherson's morning routine. Dennis was a man of carefully designed habits. Every workday morning, Monday through to Friday, he would take his brown leather briefcase, and at precisely 6.45 am, leave the red brick bungalow with its crafted veneer oak door, and walk the hundred metres or so to the bus stop. There he would wait, the briefcase always held firmly in his left hand, for the Number 231 bus. And in the evening at seven o'clock, the thin figure of Dennis would arrive back at the red brick bungalow, the briefcase still in his left hand, his day's work done.

Dennis was employed as a clerk with the City Council.This had been his job for over twenty years. His penchant for order and routine had paid off after years of diligent work. He was now Head of the Accounts Department, a position he found quite rewarding. He was forever reminding his staff that 'order is the key to a successful life', or words to that effect. He was unsure what would happen to him once he reached retirement age but he had made provisions, he assured his wife, and his pension would set the two of them free to do whatever they had always wanted, as long as it was done in an orderly fashion, of course.

The Number 231 bus was nearly always packed with sleepy workers at 6.55 am, but Dennis knew just where to position himself that he could be assured of a seat, and he was fond of telling his wife that he nearly always was able to sit in the same seat—five rows from the back, next to the side entrance of the bus, and at the window. If, for any reason, that seat was taken, Dennis preferred method of intimidation was to stare behind his rimless glasses at the occupant. This fixed gaze would result, nine times out of ten that the offending person now a trifle uncomfortable, would offer to sit somewhere else. If it happened that the person was particularly oblivious to those staring eyes of Dennis, he or she would either pretend to be asleep or lower their eyes and tinker with their mobile phone. When that happened Dennis was left standing or, if he was lucky, finding another place to sit. But both positions were uncomfortable ones for Dennis and it invariably resulted in him being in a bad mood for the rest of the day. Most people on the 231 bus at that hour knew one another, at least by sight, and Dennis being a tall thin rake of a man with a turned down mouth, was quite well known. As he was always on the 6.55 am bus to the city, Monday to Friday, it was as if his preferred seat had a huge sign on it that said, DENNIS MACPHERSON SITS HERE.

Not only was Dennis a man of immovable habits, he was also a man of fixed ideas. To argue with Dennis about any particular issue, be it political, religious or even the occasional football result, was to look at a man who had curtains in front of his eyes and the sure and certain conviction that only his opinion was the right one. There was a light bulb in the brain of Dennis, but it was turned off if anyone were to question his opinion about anything, at least that was what people said. As a consequence this intransigence made him a rather difficult person to work for and an even more awkward person to live with.

Dennis had his pet hates. Top of this list was a distrust of foreigners of any colour or creed followed closely by a hatred of tattoos, piercings or anything that disfigured, in

Dennis's opinion, the human body. But a particular hatred was reserved for the ubiquitous mobile phone, an invention he was certain was the devil's work. On the Number 231 rush hour bus, the sleepy workers often resorted to fiddling with their phones or, and this was a particular annoyance for Dennis, to see them all engaging in lengthy and private conversations on these 'instruments'. It didn't help matters at home for Dennis either. He was a father of two teenage boys, Peter and Robert, who disagreed with almost everything he said. The subject of mobile phones was a particularly sensitive issue which inevitably led to arguments. However, Dennis, being Dennis, got his own way. The mobile phone was firmly on the taboo list in the MacPherson household.

At night Dennis followed the same deadly routine on the 231 bus. At peak times in the city the weary workers resembled herds of tired and driven cattle, corralled and shunted into lines at the various bus stops. Dennis's preferred plan was to escape the initial rush and wait until the queues thinned out just enough for him to be able to get his favourite seat on the bus. To fill in time for this to happen, he often ventured into a secluded city bar for a quick glass of beer while he waited. This slight variance of character could be attributed to something within him that perhaps longed for a different life but this visit to the bar was a solitary affair for Dennis. He rarely spoke to anyone and paid for, and drank his beer, without as much as a murmur. All the barmen knew him by sight but not by name and to tell the truth, this was the way Dennis preferred it. City life affords a lot of anonymity. Dennis never had any desire to engage in idle chit chat with strangers least of all in a city bar. The one glass of beer he allowed himself was sufficient for his state of mind. If anyone had been privy to his thoughts as he sat upright on the bar stool, his right hand cradling his glass, they would have been disappointed. Dennis's thoughts were much the same as his ritualistic and dull life.

As the return journey meant that he was on the bus for an hour or so, the result was that he arrived home just after seven o'clock in the evening, five days of the week. Dennis's wife had the same penchant for order and ritual. He could expect the menu at night to be much the same, and definitely fish on Fridays.

All this looked as though it would be much the same for Dennis, day after day, until his retirement, this date so far into the future that it could be easily brushed under the carpet at the present moment, but one particular bleak winter's evening, as he waited patiently at the bus stop, the Number 231 bus did not arrive on time. The queues had thinned, and Dennis found himself standing alone, a forlorn sort of creature he looked too, with his woolly hat pulled over his ears and the collar of his coat turned up around his neck to keep out the cold. It was now half past seven and there was still no sign of the Number 231 bus.

'Hey, Mister, 'ave ya got a light?'

The voice belonged to a young man who Dennis judged to be in his mid-twenties. The man had a small gold ring pierced into his left eyebrow and a tattoo of a dragon on his neck. He held a filter tip cigarette between nicotine stained fingers.

'I don't smoke.'

The young man shrugged his shoulders.

'I'm skint. Bloody government, does bugger all for the workin' man.'

'What do you do for yourself then to get a job? I bet you're not out of bed till midday.'

The young man was the just the sort that Dennis disapproved of. Life was simple if people conducted themselves in an orderly fashion. This young man was a product of a society that had it too easy. Dennis's young life had been far from easy he felt like telling this waster. If he'd had a mother who drank too much and a father who was never there, well, this young man might have had to get out of bed and get a job like Dennis had had to do. But he thought it best not to dwell too much on that subject. He didn't like to think about those early days.

'Hey, man,' the youth said. 'What do you know? I just asked a favour from you. Don't need a lecture.'

He shook his head. Then he grinned.

'If ya waitin' for the 231 bus, it broke down. Looks like you'll be stuck in town for the night, just like me.'

This news caused Dennis to feel a spasm of anxiety that often overcome him when things didn't go according to plan.

'How do you know that?' he asked.

The young man smirked. A middle-aged couple arrived on the scene and stood politely behind Dennis. The man held a carrier bag in his right hand and the woman had her arm tucked into his. They looked as if they had waited for the bus at this stop many times. Dennis had not seen them before. He was glad of the distraction and nodded his head slightly in their direction. Neither the man nor the woman responded.

Dennis repeated his question, a little louder this time so the couple could hear.

'My girlfriend's drivin' the 231 this week. Just got a text from her to say the bus broke down at the Bridge Roundabout. They've a tow truck on the scene and the 231 won't be along for a while as they've got to go back to the depot to get another bus. She's fair cursin'. We was goin' out tonight for a pizza,' answered the young man.

'When do you think the other bus will get here?'

The woman had overhead the conversation between Dennis and the young man but without waiting for an answer, she turned to her companion and said, 'Can you ring Mary and tell her we'll be late home?' The man took out a phone from his coat pocket and started to talk to Mary. Dennis, watching all this, could feel the anxiety coming again.

'I'll find out for you, lady,' said the young man and he started to tap the screen of his phone. A few seconds later the phone made a sound.

'That's my girlfriend. Not long, about a quarter of an hour, she said. She's drivin' the new bus.' He looked at Dennis and said, 'I get to go on the bus free, ya know. The 231 is the most boring of them all. I like it when she's on the 52A, down along the river. I know all the routes but then I should do. A mechanic to trade, you know. That's where I met my girlfriend – at the bus depot.'

'That must be nice for you,' butted in the woman. She had listened to the whole conversation and found the story quite interesting.

'Yeah,' the young man replied. 'We was plannin' on gettin' hitched, ya know but then, I got made redundant a few weeks back. Cutbacks, they said an' I'd been with them about seven years. Redundancy money's not come through yet. Things a bit tight.' He looked miserable.

'That's such a shame,' said the woman. 'Isn't it, John?' she looked at her companion for an answer, but he was still busy talking to Mary.

No one spoke. The only sounds came from the swish of the cars in the street and an occasional horn blast. There was no sign of the 231.

Dennis glanced at his watch. It was now eight o'clock. He should have been home about an hour ago. His wife must be beside herself with worry, he decided, but what could he do? He felt trapped with these people.

'Here it comes,' announced the young man as the lights of a bus appeared around the corner with the magic 231 displayed above the windscreen.

'Thank goodness,' said the woman.

'About time,' grumbled her companion.

They all climbed aboard the bus, Dennis, the young man and the couple. The driver was obviously the young man's girlfriend. He hung around at the front of the bus, talking to her. Dennis found this behaviour unacceptable. He wondered should he file a complaint to the bus company. There was a big sign saying that no one should speak to the driver while the bus was in motion.

The driver didn't wait for the passengers to be seated and pulled out from the kerb in front of an oncoming vehicle. She honked the horn in an angry gesture of annoyance. The young man swayed slightly and hung onto the safety rail behind her. He said something to the driver and they both laughed. Dennis, for his part, staggered as he tried to keep from falling and headed towards his seat, five rows from the back, at the window, and found to his displeasure that this seat was already taken. A young woman sat there with a laptop on her knee. She was beautiful. Her skin as black as silk, he thought, and he forgot for one brief moment that she was sitting in 'his' seat. He wondered whether he should sit beside her but decided not to, so instead he sat on the aisle seat opposite and tried not to look at her. Quite out of the blue, he began to have rather erotic thoughts about her. He lowered his head as if to hide his feelings. He wanted to say something to her, anything would do, but she was tapping away on her laptop and appeared not to have noticed him at all. He felt rather deflated and tired all of a sudden.

The lights of the General Hospital came into view, dazzling brightness against the dark night sky. The driver braked sharply and pulled into the kerb as an ambulance passed them, its shrill siren drowning out the noise of the traffic. The young woman got up with her handbag and laptop. She smiled at Dennis. He watched her as she walked away from him. She was tall and elegant, someone you would never forget, even if you didn't know her name. Dennis watched her as she strolled towards the entrance doors of the hospital and disappeared from his sight. Then he slid across the aisle onto the seat, his seat, where she had been just a few moments before.

As the bus got further away from the city and the rows of suburban houses were visible on either side of the road, more people got off so that Dennis was left sitting by himself, and with just a few passengers on board. The young man hung onto the safety rail behind the driver and every now and then, he would lean over and say something to her. None of the other passengers seem bothered about this, except Dennis who wanted to say something to the two of them but decided not to. He would soon be off the bus and back into the safety and comfort of his own home and enjoying a hearty meal of fish and chips, the Friday menu. He could feel his mouth salivating at the thought of the food. It was more comforting to think of fish and chips than what the bus driver and her boyfriend were saying.

No neighbours looked out to see Dennis MacPherson on that Friday night for who would have thought that he would be walking past their doors at ten past nine? When he got to his home and opened the oak veneer door, all was darkness. He could feel that anxious feeling coming over him again for he had expected to see his wife, glad to have him home, and the fish and chips ready for him, but all was silent. The house felt cold and there was no sign of the cat. He turned on lights and went into the neat kitchen where all was as it always was, orderly and spotless. On the table he noticed an envelope with his name on it. He sat down. A feeling of weariness came over him, but he opened the envelope to read what was inside. There was a note in his wife's handwriting. It looked as if she had written it in a hurry.

Dennis. We waited for you but you didn't come on the 7 o'clock bus so we have had to go to the General Hospital. Your mother has had a fall. Remember that Polish girl with the tattoos that you didn't like? She found your mum in the garden and rang Peter on his phone. Apparently they have become friends??? Gran is in the hospital. We took the car. You'll have to catch the 231 back to the hospital. Robert has left you his phone to ring Peter as we don't know which ward Gran is on. He's written Peter's number down for you.

Sorry I didn't have time to make the fish tonight. X

Dennis read the note three times. Then he folded the paper neatly and placed it back into the envelope. He hadn't been to see his mother for over a year, but he remembered the Polish girl next door. She talked a lot and he disapproved of her in much the same way as he disapproved of his mother. His mother talked a lot too, especially after a few gins.

He looked at the mobile phone which lay like something alien on the table. It was strange. He picked it up. It felt weird to the touch. He turned it over, looking for numbers to press. There was nothing there except a small square hole. He ran his fingers around the instrument and stroked the front. Underneath the phone was a scrap of paper with a long number written on it. He picked that up too and studied it. Then he stared at the phone again and said out aloud:

'Now... how do I turn the wretched thing on?'

THE PERFECT MODEL

I am an artist of some renown. To me, to be an artist is the perfect occupation. Both my parents were artists. I was surrounded, in my early life, by artists and writers and craftspeople, all with varying degrees of talent. My mother told me that I could hold a pencil in my hand and make a squiggly line on a piece of paper before I could even sit up. My parents were very much in love and I was their only child. We were a tight and loving family unit.

The traditional idea of an artist, since the French Impressionist days, was one of a half-starving soul, surviving on his or her art, with a capital 'A'. This was never the case for my parents, and it definitely wasn't for me. All three of us approached the subject of art as work, and to that end, we all made a good living out of it. When it came time for me to leave the comfort of the family nest, the Art School was the destination for me. Here, I made quite a name for myself as a landscape painter. At the end of my studies at the Art School, I was fortunate to win a scholarship to travel to Italy and study the works of the Italian Renaissance masters.

In Rome, I worked hard, and it was in Rome that I met Sophia. She was the most beautiful woman I had ever seen. Her dark brown eyes seemed to look straight into your soul and I fell in love, there and then, on the very first meeting. As an artist, I was captivated by her face, perfect in proportion, and with her jet black hair that she allowed to fall onto her shoulders. Very soon, I was drawing Sophia, clothed and unclothed, and loving her. My art improved and my confidence as an artist grew. It was all to do with Sophia. She was both my soulmate and my inspiration. With Sophia beside me, I felt I could conquer any artistic world that I wanted.

We returned to Dublin as husband and wife and settled in to married life. It was fortunate for me that Sophia was also an artist, a sculptor working in bronze, miniatures of animals, in fact. Just like my mother and father, we could talk about our work, day and night. Very soon we were holding exhibitions in Dublin and London. Sophia and I were the two bright young things on the art scene. As our reputations grew, so did our finances. After ten years of marriage, we were able to afford to buy a five-bedroom mansion overlooking the sea. We attracted other artists to our home, and it seemed to us both that our good fortune would last. The only sadness between us was that we were unable to have children. It took us some time to adjust to this news, Sophia longer than me, but after a while, we were able to accept that it was not to be. We had each other and our art. That was more than so many less fortunate souls. We counted our blessings and kept working.

Our home by the sea was the perfect location for two artists in love with each other and their work. The house had many windows and, with the high ceilings and skylights in the rooms we turned into our studios, we decided that we could quite happily stay in this one place for many a long year. We loved to walk along the strand to the lighthouse which was situated a good half mile from our home. The white stone lighthouse was built at the end of the pier, positioned there as a warning light for the seas outside the harbour were treacherous. Many a ship had been wrecked on the rocks beyond the safety of the harbour. To me, this place provided all the inspiration I needed.

It had been a habit since childhood to always have my sketchpad and pencil with me. Here, facing the lighthouse, I liked to settle myself on one of the enormous rocks, take out my sketchpad and pencil and attempt to capture the scene in front of me. I loved the change of seasons, but winter was best for me. Then nature was at its most fierce. I walked as the wild weather made sitting on the rocks impossible. The ice-cold wind whipped the sea into a fury and sent the surging waves onto the walls. My eyes watered. I was a just a small speck in a dramatic landscape. Every moment the colours of the sea and sky brought subtle, then at times, dramatic changes. I could only hope to capture just a few of nature's moods, and that awareness brought a newfound humility, and I reasoned that my work could never rival the beauty I could see all around me.

Sophia joined me most days. Sometimes, she strolled alongside the wall leading to the lighthouse and she would wave. It was a reassuring signal for me to see her there. We were still very much in love.

In the summer, we decided to hold a joint exhibition of our work, and it was the lighthouse that gave me the inspiration. I would paint the scene in its many moods and Sophia, who had developed an interest in the small sea creatures that made their homes amongst the rock pools, would sculpt small bronze miniatures of these crustaceans. Our agent set to work. Very soon we had a very prestigious gallery in London agreeing to host our exhibition. We would be kept busy until then as we had just twelve months to complete the task.

It was in the autumn that my world changed forever. It had been a lovely warm day for the time of year, perfect in every way. Sea and sky dazzled me with the different shades of blue. In my mind's eye, I was intent on converting the images onto canvas, and my thoughts were far away as Sophia and I strolled back from our lighthouse walk. At the front door, Sophia stumbled and fell onto the ground. She cried out.

'Sophia!'

'It is nothing. I fall, that is all. Do not worry. I am foolish,' she said as I helped her to her feet. But I could see she was in pain.

It was then that I began to lose my beautiful Sophia. It was an inoperable cancer, the doctors said. They gave her six months.

At first, I denied that this was happening to me. After all, my world had been relatively problem free. We were the perfect couple and much admired. I went about the business of painting and tried to not see what was happening around me. Tried to pretend to myself that my beautiful Sophia was not growing weaker, day by day as the disease took hold of her, but I knew in my heart I was losing her. When the denial turned to anger, we both suffered.

'Mio caro marito', she murmured. 'Courage.'

But her words fell on deaf ears. I would have given my own life to save her. An atheist, I began to bargain my life for hers. When she was in so much pain that walking was difficult, I tried my best to comfort her. I carried her frail body to the car and drove to the lighthouse so she could see it once more. It was there, in front of the white stone building, that I decided that I would walk into the sea because I did not believe I could live without her. But I did not speak of it then. I tried my best to be cheerful for her sake, not mine. How could I let her know my anger had led me to decide on my course of action, after she had gone from me? After all, it was at the lighthouse that we had enjoyed so much of her life together.

'It is so beautiful here. I am at peace, mio caro, please believe.'

But I could not see the beauty around me anymore. I closed my artist's eyes to the world. The colours I saw then were black; a black demon had descended upon my soul, and I had not the strength of will to fight it. I no longer had any interest in my work.

'Are you painting, Philip?' Sophia asked one day, and I nodded my head.

'Ah, that is good. We have our exhibition. Lots of work to do for you, and that is, the best. I want for you to exhibit my bronzes and if they sell, the money is to go to the charity to help fight the cancer. You do this for me, sí?'

I held her hand and tried to smile. How could I tell her that I had not ventured to my studio for weeks and no colour was on the canvases?

The depression took hold and I, too, lost weight. I began to hate my life then. My artist's world had become a nightmare for me from which I could not awake, or did not want to, I was not sure of anything anymore. The comfortable existence that had been such a certainty was no longer there. I cursed my art as my darling Sophia slipped away from me.

****

121

The gallery owner came from London and begged me to exhibit. My agent despaired. My friends shook their heads.

'Sophia would have wanted you to keep going,' they said.

'I cannot live without her,' I replied.

'You must, Philip...'

No one could give me any reason why I should. The thought of walking into the sea became more appealing for me as each day took me further away from my Sophia.

One fine day I made up my mind to do it. There was no reason anymore why I had to keep on living without the woman I loved. I would walk to the lighthouse the way we used to, and sit on one of the gigantic rocks, look out towards the sea, and talk to Sophia. Then I would start walking. The last sight I would see was the white stone of the lighthouse with the dome on top of it. Its light would guide me as it had done for so many others.

I chose a time when I knew there would be no one about and the beach was quiet. I sat myself down on the rocks and looked about. To my surprise, my artist's eye, those eyes that had been blind for so long, awoke. I could see colours again, blues and greys and browns. The white of the lighthouse shimmered in front of me. I felt almost blinded by it. Then I saw the figure. She stood beside the rounded side of the lighthouse, and she waved. It was Sophia. I was certain. All thoughts of walking into the sea left me and I started to run. I clambered over the rocks, slipped and fell, but I felt no pain. I kept running along the pier towards the figure in front of me. When I got to the side of the lighthouse, there was no one there.

That evening I returned to my studio, took the virgin canvas and placed it upon my easel. The first thing I drew was a white lighthouse and beside it, I sketched the figure of a woman with long black hair and wearing a flowing red and yellow dress, my Sophia's favourite.

THE SNAKE
A Father Vic Story

It was the flies that got to Father Vic. They clung to his face in swarms. When he waved his arms around like a cowboy with a lasso, and tried to be free of their persistence, he failed, for a second or two later they were back. They crawled on his cheek; their feet seemed like glue. He muttered all sorts of expletives if he happened to be by himself. Next emotion would be anger followed just as quickly by guilt. After all, they were God's creatures and they served a purpose. Australians seemed to take no notice of them. In fact, waving them away was called "The Great Australian Salute". Father Vic admired their acceptance of what he decided was a particularly annoying adversary.

Father Vic was thinking all these things as he walked along, thinking of flies and Ireland and snakes and Mrs McNally. Father Vic remembered when he had come to this parish, on his first visit to the McNallys, the devout Catholic family with many children, how pleased he had been to find what an amazing cook Mrs McNally was. She was happy feeding her brood without murmur of complaint, and after all, the priest was just another mouth to feed. On this particular occasion, Father Vic had his eye on a particularly appealing passion fruit cake with, what he thought was, passion fruit icing. Since arriving in Australia, the priest had developed a liking for the passion fruit, never having tried that fruit before. The cake sat in the middle of the table, Mrs McNally offered him a piece; he smiled and nodded politely, his taste buds watering. She moved her hand across to cut the cake and Father Vic looked in horror as the black passion fruits moved! The flies ascended and flew off horizontally. No passion fruit, just plain icing. He took the slice, eating the cake but pushing the icing to the side of his plate. There was so much noise of children that no one noticed, but from that day on, Father Vic would examine cakes with icing of a certain variety before accepting the offering. Although, he did realise there was a certain black humour in his encounter with the passion fruit cake and would chuckle at his own foolishness.

Of course there are flies in Ireland, he thought. He recalled summers when they swarmed around the cattle and annoyed the horses. The horses twitched their tails to be rid of them. But somehow they didn't seem so invasive there — not like in Australia with its vast distances and heat and constant droughts. They were in a drought again, and times were getting harder for the farmers. It hadn't rained for six months. Father Vic remembered the rain of Ireland and how it would settle on your face like soft dew. Of course people complained about it, but they missed the rain and the constantly changing clouds and skies; they missed all that, when they were away. *Human nature being what it is*, thought the priest ruefully.

And his other unspoken fear, because he felt honour bound not to admit it, being a man of the cloth and somehow supposed to be slightly removed from other mortal's fears, but he had a fear of them and would look anxiously around when he was out walking, particularly in the heat of the day. Snakes. Of course, there were no snakes in Ireland, Saint Patrick had seen to that. The saint had supposedly sat on the top of Croagh Patrick, Ireland's

Holy Mountain, and banished them from Ireland – sent all the adders to England, perhaps?

Father Vic had climbed Croagh Patrick too, years ago. He had been eighteen and climbed for spiritual enlightenment and holy penance. Only at eighteen, it hadn't been quite that, he recalled. He had walked barefooted, the stones cut into his feet and he felt masculine bravado at his achievement, not a contrite heart. He had climbed with an old lady from Louisburgh who climbed the mountain every year saying the Rosary all the way – "Hail Mary, full of grace...," and got to the top without a sign of exhaustion or triumph as though the Lord was with her all the way. And Father Vic remembered that he had felt a tingle of shame when he looked into the old woman's eyes, looked into her eyes, and turned away.

So, flies and snakes and Ireland, and this Irish priest a long way from home. He was thinking all these thoughts more often now as he was getting older and there wasn't as much to do these days. Even the convents were closing, the nuns to be relocated in small houses, what nuns were left, that is. People didn't attend Mass as much as they used to, so Father Vic's workload was reduced somewhat. But he still liked to visit his faithful parishioners on a fairly regular basis, and that was what he was doing now, walking along the track slowly because the arthritis was in his knees. He had always enjoyed walking. He often left his car at the creek and walked the half mile to the McNally's house. They chided him for it, walking in the heat seemed an odd thing for them to understand but, after all these years, they accepted him and his Irish ways. One of them could usually spot his car parked under the shade of the old willow tree and give forewarning to the rest of the family.

But on this particular day, no one seemed to be about and the half mile seemed long and Father Vic began to wonder, along with the snakes and the flies and the state of the church in the modern world, if he should perhaps start driving right up to the door of the McNally's house in the future.

He was thinking all this when suddenly, and completely unexpectedly, he was stopped by a young aboriginal girl of about ten years of age who appeared like an apparition out of nowhere and put her hand on his arm to stop him walking any further. Father Vic looked a little bemused but smiled, nevertheless, as was his nature.

'Hello there,' he said. 'What can I do for you?' because in truth, he didn't know what else to say. She didn't speak but held onto the priest's arm so as to prevent his moving.

Father Vic vaguely remembered who she was. There weren't many indigenous folk in the area. Only two families who lived a few miles away. The children attended school in rather an erratic way. Then the families would wander off, go "walkabout" and be gone for months on end. They lived a separate existence from the rest of the community, "marginalized", Father Vic thought the new "buzz" word was, but he never seemed to be able to penetrate into their circle, so seeing this young girl in his pathway somewhat unnerved him. She was barefoot, her shorts and tee-shirt well washed, her black hair uncombed, her black eyes never moving from Father Vic's face.

All this seemed to take forever, this moment in time, and then the girl pointed towards a scrubby bush on the dusty ground. Father Vic looked in the direction of the pointing finger and saw nothing. The ground was bone dry, lack of rain had caused cracks to appear in the soil and when you walked, you left a trail of dusty footprints on the ground. Father Vic was about to say something to the effect that he had better be on his way as he was due at the McNallys any minute now, when he saw what he was supposed to be seeing, and seeing the object caused his heart to pump wildly and his mouth to turn dry. What was lying under the bush, brown as the ground on which it lay and coiled around so as not to know its size, was a brown snake, its scales glistening in the midday sun.

A few steps further and Father Vic, with his mind so far away, would have stepped on the creature. He felt a moment of sheer panic, felt the urge to run – run back to the safety of his car – run away from priestly duties, run and hide, like a little boy, so he could not be in any danger again from this animal or from this country with its heat and drought and flies. An irrational moment the priest knew. The next moment, he felt ashamed of his own cowardice.

This little girl had saved him by her awareness. This was her country, these were her creatures. She showed no fear of snakes, was untroubled by flies. The two of them stood, motionless, and watched the snake. It sensed the danger of humans so close by, uncoiled its vast body and moved towards them. Father Vic, the palms of his hands now wringing with sweat and with droplets of perspiration on his forehead, watched as if this was happening to someone else. He could see the snake's tongue, sliding in and out, exploring and examining, what was in its path. If Father Vic had had a stick he would have attempted to kill, to bring the stick down hard onto the snake's head, crush its face, break it and leave it dead; never then would it move again. He would have killed it and been proud of his bravery. But he had no stick and no weapon and only a young black girl beside him who had no fear and wished the creature no harm.

The two of them, standing completely still, watched as the snake slid slowly away and out of sight leaving a track in the dusty ground as evidence of its passing. The priest put his hand on the girl's shoulder and spluttered a "thank you" and at his words, she turned, removing her hand from his arm, turned to look straight at him, and smiled, her white teeth so white in her black face. This girl looked at Father Vic in such a way that he recalled the old woman climbing Croagh Patrick in Ireland all those years ago. The same look, unexplainable, but the look of wisdom from a soul unfettered to things temporal, and the priest, who was a good man despite all his human frailties, felt somehow chastened. He put his hand on the dark head and blessed her in his thoughts and in so doing, wondered if perhaps it was she who should be doing the blessing for him.

At that, he smiled to himself and went on his way, a slightly wiser man for the encounter.

'After all that, we've forgotten the butter!' exclaimed Joan Anderson with a slight chuckle.

Her sister, Mildred, eight years older at seventy-five and already showing signs of the greater age, looked up from her picnic basket.

'Well, really Joan... that was your department.'

Joan giggled. 'We always seem to forget something. It's always such a rush to get away. Remember the time we went to Cornwall for the week and forgot to pack toothbrushes. You were so cross.'

'Well, it seems such a little thing to be organised. Once one has a system, everything else is easy.'

She sighed. A lifetime of working in the Civil Service had given her a penchant for order, and she liked everything to be 'just so.' Her father had been like that too, and she could remember him as though it was yesterday saying, 'Mildred, there's a place for everything and everything in its place. Never forget that.' She never had. *It's a pity Joan hadn't listened to him a bit more*, she thought crossly, but then Joan never listened to anything and always did just what she wanted.

The two sisters finished the rest of their unpacking in silence. Years of living together had established a routine for them in everything they did. *Mildred was right*, Joan thought. The butter was her department. Joan always packed the food in the picnic hamper – plates, cups, cutlery, Thermos flask, bread and cakes. They liked to make their own sandwiches when they got to their picnic spots. Mildred always said they tasted better freshly made and so that was an established procedure. Mildred did the driving so everything pertaining to the car was her responsibility. She loved to put her foot down and watch the speedo clock climb up and up. She often thought if she'd been a man, she would have been a racing driver. The combination of speed and danger rather appealed to the other side of her nature. *The side she got from her mother*, she thought. Her mother was full of fanciful schemes and was forever dashing of on some project or other. *I don't know how Father put up with it*, thought Mildred to herself, *but then, he didn't really. Well, mustn't think about that, it's all in the past now and best forgotten.* She looked up at Joan who was pouring out the tea.

'Do you think we could let Nipper have a little run? It's quiet enough here.'

Nipper was their pet cocker spaniel and much loved by the two sisters. Joan clapped her hands together, a little habit she had when she got excited.

'Oh, yes, let's,' she said. 'He'll come back. Here, Nipper. Come here, boy.'

She took Nipper's lead and unhooked it from his collar. Nipper shook himself with delight and bounded off in the direction of the river.

'Now, you come back when we call. And don't go far away.' Joan called out to him as the dog disappeared behind a clump of bushes.

It was a lovely May day; just right for a picnic. There wasn't a cloud in the sky and the sun was warm enough for the time of year. Everything had a clear freshness about it and spring was in the air. The two women sat sipping their tea and eating their sandwiches, each thinking their own thoughts and enjoying the day and the feeling of being out in the open air. They lived in the house they had inherited from their parents in a little village eight miles from 'their' picnic spot. They liked to think of the picnic spot as theirs because they felt they had discovered it. Not that they minded other people coming to it but they enjoyed being on their own and never went there in the summer when it got crowded around the river. 'It's just not the same,' Mildred would say and they would spend more time in their own garden during the long summer days.

Mildred was thinking of the garden as she sat sipping her tea. She was intending to plant a row of sweet peas this year along the back fence. She liked the flowers but had never really got round to growing them in her own garden so this year she thought she would make an extra effort. Joan didn't bother much about the garden. Flowers never really interested her much, but she was keen on her small vegetable patch and proud of her tomatoes which she grew in her tiny glasshouse. Joan would develop an interest in things and just as quickly drop it. A grasshopper mind, Mildred used to tell her, but Joan never seemed to take much notice. They got on well enough, but Mildred sometimes wished that Joan wasn't quite so flighty. *It had got her into all manner of trouble in her life,* she thought.

'Mildred, do you think we could invite the Johnsons over for tea one day? They're such a nice couple and Mr Johnson lent me that book about Zurich.'

The Johnsons were a retired couple who had recently moved into the village. Joan was delighted to learn that they spent their holidays in Switzerland – a place that had a special meaning for Joan who had done a lot of travelling in her life and loved recapturing all the memories of her journeys. The Johnsons had lived in many of the places that Joan had visited, and they loved comparing notes.

Mildred looked a bit cross. 'Well, I suppose so,' she said, 'but really I don't' know what you see in them. He does all the talking and she just sits there. You know I don't like men who ignore their wives.'

'Oh, you're forever going on about that, Mildred. She's nice when you get to know her,' Joan concluded, and she gave her sister a rather superior look.

'And I suppose you know her, do you?'

'Well, I've met her a few times in the village.'

'You never told me that.'

'Have I got to tell you everything?' Joan answered and she glared at Mildred.

Mildred was used to this tactic and she pounced on her younger sister: 'It's been my experience that you never tell me everything. You've been like that all your life.'

Joan pouted.' Well, every time I even attempt to tell you something, you're always telling me I'm wrong.'

Mildred said nothing. There was silence for a few moments as each woman decided on the next line of attack. It was Joan who spoke finally.

'Anyway, I can tell you something about the Johnsons.'

Mildred smiled coldly. 'What possible interest could I have in the Johnsons? I've told you, I don't like the way he carries on... and I don't know her as well as you appear to. What about them?'

Joan sensed victory and pursed her lips.

'They know someone you know... or used to know.'

'Joan, this is ridiculous. Why must you always have these little games? You're just like Mother, you know how her behaviour used to vex Father... 'Mildred put her hand over her mouth. 'I'm sorry, I didn't mean to bring it up but you really go on and on.'

Joan got up and started to put the plates and cups into the hamper. She grabbed the Thermos flask and shoved it furiously in beside the cups.

'Alright, Joan, I'm sorry. It was wrong of me to say that. Am I forgiven?'

Joan looked up and glared at her sister. 'I suppose so,' she said.

'Now,' murmured Mildred, soothingly, 'what about the Johnsons?'

'They knew Anthony Phillips in Zurich.'

There are occasions in everyone's life when the word of another person spoken at an unexpected time can cause a shock that sometimes seems to freeze time. This was just such an occasion for Mildred. She stared stupidly at her sister. A moment before this remark, she had been in the process of getting up to help with the clearing away of the picnic things. She sank back onto her foldup chair as though she had been mortally wounded. Nipper decided to arrive back at this precise moment, and Joan knelt down to fuss over him. She seemed oblivious to the effect that her remark had made on her sister. Mildred finally spoke.

'How could they know him?'

'Well, we always knew he went to the Continent. Father told us that.'

'But, Joan... how could they know him? He must be nearly ninety.'

'Oh, it was years ago,' Joan replied airily. 'You know, the Johnsons lived in Zurich for two years. Remember, they used to go to that same little Italian restaurant that

Anne and I discovered when we had our holiday there. What year was that...?

'Never mind. What was he doing?'

'Who?'

Mildred seemed to have difficulty saying the words. 'Anthony Phillips', she said at last.

'Well, English people tend to meet one another in foreign parts. I was forever running into people I knew back home... so I guess they just moved in the same circle and met him that way. It's a small world, isn't it?'

'I don't think I'll ever be able to look at the Johnsons again. How could you think of bringing them into our house... Father's house?'

'Well, that's just silly, Mildred. The Johnsons are such nice people.'

Mildred got up and grabbed her sister by the shoulders and shook her.

'Can't you stop saying how nice the Johnsons are?' she yelled. 'How could we ever live it down if they found out?'

The two women looked at each other.

'He had a woman with him.' Joan said after a few moments.

'When?'

'In Zurich... when the Johnsons met him.'

'Have you been discussing *everything* with the Johnsons? Really, Joan...'

No, of course not. Mr Johnson just happened to mention it, that's all. I don't think they know anything... anything about the other...'

'You only think?' Mildred was furious.

'Alright, Mildred, they know nothing. Only that he was well and seemed to be living a good life, and the woman was American.'

'American?'

'Yes. From Chicago, I think.'

'Were they married?'

'I didn't ask. I didn't like to talk about it. They said he had a very nice home and seemed rather well off.'

'That would be a change,' said Mildred.'

Joan looked at Mildred and put her arm around her shoulders.

'I'm sorry, Millie. I didn't know how to tell you. But it is strange, isn't it? It was just by accident that I brought up his name.'

'How?'

Well, I just happened to say one day that I had been to Zurich and then we talked about that little Italian restaurant and I said something about the paintings that they had on the wall... it was quite a feature of the place... and then we started to talk about art... and artists... and quite out of the blue, they said they knew an English artist once in Zurich and I said, "Oh, really?" and Mr Johnson said, "Yes, I don't suppose you've ever heard of him, Phillips, Anthony Phillips." Mildred, I nearly went through the ground. Can you imagine it? Of all the people in the world! "What a coincidence," I said, trying to keep calm. "I have heard the name. Did you know him well?" "Oh, fairly well," says Mr Johnson," he and Barbara kept in touch for quite a bit after we left Zurich. We don't hear much from them now, though. It's been years." That's how I heard about the American woman, Mildred.' Joan concluded with a grimace.

Mildred didn't answer.

'Anyway,' Joan concluded, 'it's been all so long ago. He's probably dead by now. As you say, he must be at least ninety, probably closer to ninety-five.'

'This has been a big shock for me, Joan. I do think you could have told me before this. Why did you have to leave to tell me on our picnic? You know how I enjoy these outings. And now look what you've done. Gone and spoilt everything. You always manage to ruin everything I've ever wanted... or done.'

Joan stamped her feet. 'Mildred, that's not fair. I wanted to tell you but every time I mentioned the Johnsons...'

Mildred interrupted. 'How was I to know they would know Anthony Phillips? Really, Joan, you could have been more considerate.'

'Oh, Millie, don't be so cross. Nipper can't make out what's happening, can you, Nipper?'

At this bit of attention, Nipper wagged his tail and looked from one to the other. Joan patted him on his head, and the dog jumped up, pushing his front paws onto Joan's knees. Mildred managed a smile at his antics.

'You do spoil that dog, don't you?'

Joan giggled. 'I'm not the only one. He knows he has the two of us where he wants us, don't you, darling?'

Nipped woofed affirmatively.

Mildred carried the fold-up chair to the back of the car. She always did the packing as she said that Joan didn't have a clue and was inclined to leave things behind. Joan did the cooking and Mildred cleared up. Their lives never varied much now nor would they have wanted any change. *Leave that to the young,* Mildred thought. She finished the tidying up and wandered down to the river where Joan was sitting on a rock, thoughtfully looking over to the distant hills.

'I guess we'd be better heading back soon,' Mildred said.

'Yes', answered Joan.

'Is anything wrong?'

'No... I was just thinking, Millie, there's something I've always wanted to ask... I just don't know how to put it.'

'Well, you've certainly said enough today.'

'I know... and it's to do with that. So, I guess it's the right time to ask.'

'Well?'

'I know it's a long time ago... and you needn't tell me if you don't want to... but... Mildred, were you in love with Anthony Phillips?'

'I don't know what that's got to do with anything.'

'I'm sorry. I won't say another word about it if you don't' want to tell me. It's just that... I often thought you were.'

Mildred looked at her sister and sighed.

'Well, I don't suppose it matters now. We're both getting old, aren't we? The answer to your question is "yes", and he made it impossible for me to love anyone else.'

'Ah... I thought as much,' said Joan, triumphantly.

'Well, there's no need to be like that. He didn't love me, you know that, don't you?'

Joan blushed. 'Yes,' she said.

'Anthony Phillips only loved one person and that was Anthony Phillips.'

'And Mother,' Joan said, quietly.

The two women were silent for a few moments and then Mildred spoke.

'Ah, yes. I guess he did love her. She certainly gave up everything for him. Father, her home, her country... us.'

'I wonder did she ever regret it?'

'I don't know. It all happened so quickly. It was my first year in the Civil Service, remember? I came home one weekend and she was gone.'

'I was at St. Catherine's. You know, you told me when I came home at mid-term.'

'Father and I felt it was better to leave it and tell you to your face. You couldn't write that sort of thing in a letter.'

'No.'

'I can remember him so vividly, Joan. He was everything I thought a man should be. I was jealous of Mother. I guess I sensed there was something between them, but I wouldn't believe it for a long time after. It's brought it all back to me, you talking about him today. I just wouldn't want the Johnsons to suspect anything. We've kept it hidden all these years.'

'I know, Mildred. Do you think she was happy?'

'Happy? Really, you do go on with such fanciful notions sometimes. Happiness? What's happiness? If she thought she was happy running off with a man and leaving her husband and children and dying in some god-forsaken spot, well, she was welcome to it. That was her trouble. Always thinking she wanted something else in life... jumping from one thing to another. Why, Father was the kindest of men. It broke his heart. I wouldn't want that on my conscience. She left our father for some fancy artist who ends up living in Zurich with an American! I could have told her he'd come to no good. Well, really, Joan...

look at the time. We must be heading back. It'll be dark soon and you know I don't like driving at night now. Come on.'

Joan got up from the rock and the two women and Nipper walked slowly back to the car.

'Mildred...?'

'What is it now, Joan?'

'We will be able to have the Johnsons over for tea, won't we?'

Well, really, Joan... you are the most impossible of women!' Mildred paused. Then she said in a quiet voice. 'Oh, I suppose so, if you must... but we won't mention our little secret, will we?'

THE TROPHY

I often wondered over the years what had happened to Amanda Caldethorpe, the star of our Ada Vale Squash Club. My last memory of Amanda was when she hit the winning shot high over the head of her opponent and won both the match and the trophy for our team, the Rockets. At long last, we had defeated the Moonwalkers, our rivals of many a tournament, and the four of us girls felt the jubilation and the intoxication of victory.

Of course, it was Amanda who had won the trophy for us. She was a formidable and aggressive player – we always left her to play the last game. Her speed and agility were legend. At twenty-nine, she was married to John, I think that was his name, and had a comfortable four-bedroom house in the suburbs. No children and no prospect of them as Amanda seemed a bit 'anti' reproducing. The husband was away a lot on business which always gave us cause for a lot of giggles at Amanda's expense. Women will be women.

Anyway, on this particular triumphant day, as I recall, Amanda, tall, blonde and beautiful, had been quite talkative. I knew that she had been determined to win that trophy. With her victory, she gained not only the trophy for her team but also the trophy for the best overall player in the tournament. She was well pleased with herself.

Not that she didn't have enough trophies. My friend, Cynthia, who had been to her house, told me that a whole wall in the living room was devoted to evidence of Amanda's prowess on the squash court.

'Amazing, it was,' Cynthia told me. 'There were cups and trophies and medals. And she's won badminton trophies too.'

'How does she find the time?' I quizzed, suitably impressed.

Amanda was definitely something else. I remember that day. Just as she came off the court, flushed with excitement, sweat pouring from her face and her blue top clinging provocatively to her body, showing the shape of her breasts to perfection, Andrew Pearson appeared as if from nowhere to congratulate her, and us, of course. We had played the final round of the competition at our own club, Ada Vale, and Andrew was the manager there. Now if the truth be known, we girls had many a secret erotic thought about Andrew Pearson. He was male body supreme. He seemed to have muscles stacked on muscles. An Adonis, he kept himself in superb physical condition at the squash court, the gym and the swimming pool. Andrew Pearson was our collective fantasy, and we spent a fair amount of time speculating about him. There didn't seem to be a Mrs Pearson, so we knew he was available, but, as all of us were reasonably happily married women, it really wasn't an option. But we could still wonder.

Anyway, the day of the Finals, I remember that Andrew Pearson was as elated as we were about our victory which would mean kudos for him as well as the Ada Vale Squash Club. We could be assured of our photo in the local paper when we were duly presented with our trophies, so there would be handshakes and kisses all round. Getting a quick peck on the cheek from Andrew Pearson was worth winning the tournament for, although we all agreed that most of the congratulations belonged to Amanda, and rightly so.

We were surprised a few weeks later when Amanda didn't turn up at the Presentation of Trophies Dinner and nor did her husband, John. But Andrew Pearson was there and got his photo taken with our team. We all smiled for the camera. Then Andrew gave us a quick kiss and a handshake, much to our delight. He really was something.

Amanda's trophy for the *Best Player of the Season* was indeed beautiful. My friend, Cynthia went up to receive it for Amanda. The trophy consisted of two polished pieces of mahogany about twenty centimetres high on a mahogany base and a rectangular silver insert between the two pieces of wood with *Best Player of the Year* engraved in the centre. All the names of the past prize winners and the year they won were there; Amanda's name as well. To add a touch of class, two stylised squash rackets also made of silver were set into the wood on either side. It was exquisite. Our smaller trophy, a silver cup, didn't receive anything like the interest that Amanda's did.

I remember the night ended with Andrew Pearson saying that he would give the trophy to Amanda as he knew where she lived.

That year was the Rockets greatest year because soon after that I suffered a knee injury and had to stop playing squash for a while. Cynthia moved away and I really had nothing more to do with the Ada Vale Squash Club until a few years later when I happened to be on the other side of town.

A new shopping centre had opened, and I thought I would nip into the supermarket and pick up a few items for the family dinner. Imagine my astonishment when I came up the aisle past the cornflakes and saw Amanda Caldethorpe pushing her trolley. Well, Amanda wasn't exactly pushing it. A small boy was trying to do it for her.

'Amanda', I blurted out, 'fancy seeing you here.'

'Goodness', she replied, 'how long is it? I haven't seen you since...?' I sensed she was struggling.

'Since we won the tournament, remember? Against the Moonwalkers.'

'Oh, of course. How time flies.'

'Is this your little boy?' I asked, looking down at the small, curly-haired little boy who must have been between four and five.

'Oh yes,' said Amanda, putting her hand on the child's head. 'This is Sam.'

'Hello, Sam.'

I smiled at the little lad, and then I said to Amanda. 'Your husband must be delighted.'

I remembered how long they seemed to be without any children and how distant Amanda had been about the subject.

'Well...' Amanda hesitated, 'this isn't John's.'

I must have turned beetroot red with embarrassment, completely at a loss for words.

'Sam's Daddy is Andrew Pearson.' And she ruffled Sam's hair as she said the words.

'Oh!'

'Remember that day we won the tournament?'

I nodded. Words had failed me. Here was Amanda, still blonde, beautiful and athletic, and not in the least concerned about my obvious embarrassment.

'Well, Andrew and I sort of got together that day.'

I wished the ground would sink beneath me, but Amanda was smiling with a far-off look, her eyes fixed on some distant memory. She grinned.

'Oh, by the way,' she said in an offhand sort of way, 'John and I divorced after that. Andrew and I got married last year, and we have opened our own squash centre at Blythe Heights. You could always come over for a game if you like.'

I could feel my face turning redder and redder as she spoke. Amanda took a packet of cornflakes off the shelf and threw them into her shopping trolley.

'Oh well, must be off now,' she said, and she grinned again showing off that perfect set of white teeth. It was a devilish sort of grin, and I wondered what she was thinking about.

'You know,' she said, 'Andrew and I often joke about the night of the presentation do. He says I got two trophies that night!'

I watched her walk along the aisle with Sam still trying to push the trolley. She turned and waved to me. Then she disappeared from my sight. I finished my shopping rather quickly after that. It was only after I got home that I had a thought. Maybe Amanda wasn't so bad after all? I might just go to her squash centre. It would be fun to see her and Andrew Pearson together again. Perhaps there would be a few more trophies on display?

THE TRIUMPH OF LOUISA RIDGEWAY

Everyone has a past. Everyone has secrets. Forty-one-year-old Louisa Ridgeway had a dark past, and an even darker secret.

One sunny October day Louisa was out walking with her cocker spaniel, Puddles, and she happened to spy a figure she thought she would never see again. At first she wasn't absolutely certain that it was who she thought it was. She put her head down and tried to walk faster to avoid any contact. For ten years Louisa had hoped that she would never meet this man ever again. He was a part of a dark past, and if, on occasion, without warning, thoughts of him came into her mind, she brushed those demons away like leaves in the wind. Knowing there was no way to avoid him now, Louisa gripped Puddle's lead hard in her right hand and prepared herself for the inevitable.

It was him. She was certain now and her heart beat faster. Puddles stiffened, and the hairs rose on his back as the man got closer to them. The dog growled slightly. This was a surprise. Most times, Puddles was a happy-go-lucky sort of dog and of a friendly nature.

'Well, well,' the man said when the two of them were just a few paces from each other. 'Fancy meeting you again after all these years... Magda.'

'You must be mistaken. That's not my name...'

'Ah, we both know that's not true. Let's find a park bench and talk.'

'What do you want?'

'To talk.'

Now Louisa knew that this wasn't a chance meeting at all. He had been waiting for her. She wanted to be anywhere other than the present moment. She felt vulnerable like a frightened and cornered animal and wished there was somewhere to hide, but there was nowhere. The park was open parkland with manicured gardens and shady trees. People were walking about, enjoying the day.

'You are looking well, Magda,' the man said when the two of them sat down on the park bench.

Louisa felt like saying that the man didn't look in the same healthy condition, but she decided not to. So she just said, 'I am not Magda. You know my name. It's Louisa.'

'Of course, that's the name you are called by now, Louisa Ridgeway. To me though, you are always Magda. Magda Kawinski.' He smiled with his lips, but his eyes were cold and his face was the grey of death. This man was ill.

'Tell me what you want. I need to get back home.'

'All in good time. It's a nice day to meet old friends.'

'You were never really my friend.'

'Ah, Magda, you were always a fighter. That's why you were so good at your job.'

'That's in the past. You told me that. That was the agreement.'

The same smile on his lips as he said, 'But you know, Magda, that is not true. There's no escape for any of us.'

'I have a husband, children. You know that.'

'Of course I know. It was all arranged. You are happy then? The years have been good for you, I can see that.'

There was silence between them; the kind of uncomfortable silence that often occurs between people who were once friends and meet again as strangers. Then the man said,

'We are one and the same, isn't that true, Magda? We both have our secrets, don't we now?'

****

The baby was wrapped in a woman's grey fleeced jacket and left at the top of the stairs. There was blood on the sleeve of the jacket and the cold and naked baby cried. The first person to pick the small bundle up and into her arms was the Polish nurse, Magda Kawinski. Tears came into Magda's eyes as she held the tiny human soul close to the warmth of her breast, for the nurse had seen babies die in Poland.

The nurses looked after the tiny baby as best they could, but it was Magda Kawinski who cared the most. Magda would have liked to keep the baby, but it was an impossible situation for the kind and motherly woman had six children of her own. Money was tight in the family home; another mouth to feed would be too much. But this nameless soul should have a name. The nurses decided to call the baby Magda Kawinski, and this was the name on her Birth Certificate. It was indeed possible that the Polish nurse was the only person in the world who truly and unconditionally loved the abandoned infant, if only for a brief period of time. Such was the beginning of the life of the woman who would become Louisa Ridgeway.

The young Magda survived her childhood for she was a fighter and a survivor. But deep down the loneliness of the loss of identity and with that, a real family, was like a cloak that she wore that covered her from head to toe. There were foster parents who were kind and others who were not. She made up an identity. Her parents were Polish. She tried to learn the language to help make it real. With her black hair and deep brown eyes, she could easily assume that role. Her mother and father had been killed in a car accident, she told people, and her aunts and uncles were still living in Poland. A lie often told becomes, in time, truth to the teller. One day Magda took a map of Poland, closed her eyes and with her index finger jabbed it onto the map. When she opened her eyes, she saw the name of a small Polish village near to the German border. This is where her aunts and uncles lived. She read the village name out aloud, and in time could pronounce the name as fluently as if she were a native. This connection to a fictional family was a comfort to the lonely Magda, and it was to sustain her throughout her troubled childhood and adolescence.

When she was eighteen she got a job as a sales assistant in a small department store in the city and for the first time Magda felt she belonged somewhere. The other workers were kind to her, and even though it was just an eight-hour kindness, it was something. It was here that she met Janet, five years older than Magda, with long auburn hair to her shoulders and a face full of freckles. It was Janet who was to introduce the lonely and vulnerable orphan into a shadowy world, a world that included luxuries that could only be dreamed of, and a lifestyle so totally different from what she had known. False friends are false hopes. Many years later Magda was to learn this lesson, and in a painful way, but for the meantime, she and Janet became inseparable.

'There's someone I'd like you to meet,' Janet said to her one day when the two of them were sitting side by side in the park eating their lunch.

'Sounds interesting,' replied Magda and took a bite out of her apple.

'He's asked to meet you, by the way.'

'Now I'm intrigued. Who would want to meet me? Who is he?'

'His name is Miles Campbell and he has asked us to meet him in Clancy's wine bar this Friday night at seven, after work. I said you'd be able to come.'

'What's he like?'

'Wait and see, Magda… wait and see.'

Miles Campbell was nothing like Magda had imagined. He was about forty years of age and it became evident to Magda in a very short time that Miles and Janet were in some sort of relationship. Miles wore an expensive suit, and his soft hands with their manicured nails had not seen physical work. He bought a bottle of the finest Chardonnay, and the three of them perched on plush leather chairs at the end of the bar. The bartender left them alone. He seemed to know Miles and Janet. It was obvious that they had been to Clancy's before. When they left the bar, Miles took hold of Magda's hand and held it for a few seconds before he let it go. He smiled and then he said,

'We'll meet up again, Magda. Next Friday? At Clancy's?'

The words were said in such a way as to be a command. Magda felt her cheeks redden but she nodded her head.

It became a regular thing for the three of them to go to Clancy's on Friday nights and all the time Janet kept silent about Miles. But one day, three months after the three of them had become friends, she said to Magda, completely out of the blue,

'Miles is a union official. Rather high up I think... but he doesn't talk about his work... just thought you might like to know what he does.'

This was a surprise to Magda. She found it rather intriguing that the well-dressed man with the manicured nails could be involved with a workers' union.

'How did you ever get to meet him then?' Magda was curious. She and Janet had become closer. Janet was almost like a sister to Magda these days. Janet just shrugged her shoulders.

'Just happened to be there at the right time and place, I guess,' she said.

'I'd never have guessed that Miles would have anything to do with helping the working class. Well, he's not like us, is he? Looks like he's got plenty of money to splash around.'

'There's a lot you don't know', replied Janet and she was silent.

A few weeks after this conversation Miles invited the girls to Domingo's for a meal instead of going to Clancy's wine bar on the Friday night. Domingo's was the most expensive restaurant in town. Never in a million years had Magda expected ever to set foot in the place. She wore her best dress and with her black hair, in curls and falling softly onto her shoulders, she really was quite beautiful. This did not pass unnoticed with Miles.

'Magda, what a lovely sight you are tonight,' he said, and he glanced towards Janet who was poker-faced and very quiet. 'I'm a lucky man to have such beautiful girls to accompany me. Now, let's see what Domingo's has to offer... I can recommend the steaks.'

The waiter seemed to know Miles and Janet. He hovered around their table in a way that suggested he expected a rather generous tip. Magda, for her part was rather overwhelmed by it all. She tried to hide her embarrassment at not knowing which piece of cutlery to choose by lowering her head and fumbling with her table napkin. The waiter had made such a fuss of unfolding the napkin and placing it on her lap. The lonely Magda had never known such attention. She felt completely out of her depth in the swanky restaurant and barely listened to the conversation between Miles and Janet. At the end of the meal, Miles asked for the bill, paid by credit card and left a generous tip for the waiter. The waiter bowed to the three of them in a rather servile manner which Magda found rather embarrassing. As they left the restaurant, Miles put his arm around Magda's waist in a familiar gesture and said to her,

'I'd like you to join me next Saturday at my place, Magda. There's someone I think you'd like to meet.' He winked at Janet who remained silent. Again, it was impossible to refuse any of Miles's invitations and Magda, seduced by the attention that this well-dressed man bestowed upon her, nodded her head in agreement.

'Thank you, Miles,' she said, and she coughed ever so slightly to hide her embarrassment, once again.

****

When Magda and Janet arrived at Miles's rather pretentious house set in a three-acre garden with an outdoor swimming pool and tennis court, people were already mingling around the barbeque area. Magda felt out of place, awkward and shy, but when Miles came towards her, hand outstretched, her shyness disappeared. She was so under the spell of Miles. It seemed he could do no wrong. There was someone he wanted her to meet. That person was Russell, a young man of about twenty with a shock of red hair and blue eyes that seemed perpetually worried. It turned out that Russell was a student, an activist and a revolutionary, and when his eyes met the dark brown eyes of Magda, she felt that she had fallen in love. It all started out in such an innocent fashion. Very soon the two of them were lovers, and when Janet casually remarked one Friday evening at Clancy's, that it might be an idea to find out what young Russell was planning, Miles nodded his head and said that would be a good idea. So the innocent Magda agreed without any more persuasion. Very soon she was telling Miles everything that Russell was up to, and when a demonstration was in the offing, all banner waving and revolutionary, Miles, the trade union man, was the first to know the secret plans. After all, Magda, who had no political leaning whatsoever, thought that this would be of great interest to Miles. It was.

Russell and Magda were lovers for six months and then one day, he disappeared. Magda was beside herself with worry but when she asked Miles and Janet about Russell, both were silent. It was as if they had never met the young man. Magda dried her eyes and was glad that at least she had the two of them. A few months later Magda was to meet someone whom she always thought of as the love of her life, and again, it was Miles who introduced her to him. Josh Finlayson was a trade union man, just like Miles, only Josh was clever and had the eyes of a revolutionary and the charisma of a leader. He was often in the news and when he spoke, people listened.

Magda fantasised that one day she would marry Josh and they would have a house in the suburbs and two point four children and become so very ordinary. People would think they were boring and somehow this boringness would make up for the lost and lonely years. The months went past, but Josh never spoke to her of a future together. Instead, his whole focus was on trying to change the system to make things better for the working classes who had been exploited throughout history but on whom the ruling class relied so heavily for their own well-being. The workers had been duped, he told her, but once enough of them woke up, it would be a new world.

'Does Miles think the same way as you?' Magda asked him one day after Josh had spent half an hour discussing the overthrowing of the system and how it could be done. 'He asked me the other day about the office workers' strike.'

The office workers at Magda's department store were up in arms about a pay deal and there were rumblings of a strike.

'Miles has his own agenda,' was the reply.

'What do you mean?'

'Just that, Magda.'

Josh frowned and ran his fingers through his hair. Any time he did this, Magda wasn't sure what he was thinking, and this made her cross. She couldn't imagine a life without Miles in it. Miles had become her mentor and her friend. She trusted Miles, perhaps even more than Josh.

'I like Miles, that's all,' she said.

'I know you do, Magda', Josh replied. 'Be careful, that's all.'

'Whatever do you mean?'

'Let's change the subject. How about going out for a walk? Clear the head.'

He gave her a playful tickle and she forgot all about Miles and the working classes, everything, in fact, but Josh.

Their relationship continued for another six months. Throughout this time the Friday night meet up with Miles and Janet at Clancy's, or sometimes at Domingo's, became such a regular thing that Magda couldn't imagine there being an end to it. The orphan had found a family and, with Josh, the hope that one day this family thing could become real.

One evening, when the three of them were at Clancy's wine bar, the conversation got round to Josh and in an altogether casual way. Magda, in love, was glad to tell all. She hardly noticed the look that passed between Miles and Janet.

'Josh suffers from insomnia,' she blurted out. 'He has so much going on in his head. Sometimes I wake up and he's nowhere to be seen. I worry about him then. He works too hard and thinks too much.'

'That's not good,' said Miles. He put his hand on Magda's. 'I have a friend,' he continued, 'a doctor; he could prescribe some sleeping pills which might help. You could give them to him. I know Josh is dedicated and takes his work home with him. We both know he wouldn't go near doctors, but you could slip the pills into his bedtime drink and he'd never know. Might give you a good sleep too... if Josh wasn't pacing the floor.' He chuckled.

'Why, that sounds a good idea, Miles. Anything I could do to help him the better.' She paused. 'The pills might get rid of his headaches too, if he could get a good night's sleep. Yes, I'll try that. I think that would help Josh. If you could get me some pills, I'll do it.'

****

The police were called, and the coroner thought Josh's death was suspicious. Magda, overcome with the loss and distraught, turned once again to Miles. He was the rock to whom she clung to like some poor shipwrecked soul.

'There is nothing for you to worry about, Magda, dear,' was Miles's response. 'You aren't guilty of anything. The police are only doing their job.'

'But I gave him the pills...?'

Miles laughed.

'Oh, Magda,' he said. 'They were just ordinary old sleeping pills. You did nothing wrong. I'm sorry about Josh. We all know he worked too hard. Burned himself out and his health suffered. Such a shame for one so young but life has to go on, doesn't it? He would have wanted it. He wouldn't have wanted you to give up, now would he?'

Magda, through eyes filled with tears, nodded.

'There's something else though.' Miles took her hand in his.

'What?'

'I've got some good news for you now. There's an opportunity for you to go to Amarillo, Texas, triple your salary, accommodation, meet new people, make a new start. What do you think? And there's something else too.'

'What do you mean, an opportunity? I've never been anywhere much. Texas is so far away.'

'Janet has offered to go with you,' Miles said. 'She's ready to have an adventure too. And after all, you both said your job at the department store can get rather boring, now haven't you?'

156

'I don't understand.'

'You will, Magda. All in good time... and Janet will be there with you. Don't think too long though.'

Magda frowned.

'You said there was something else?'

'There is.'

Miles took an envelope from the inside pocket of his jacket and laid it on the table.

'Open it,' he said.

Magda slid her finger along the fold and took out an air ticket to Amarillo, Texas.

'What does this mean?'

It didn't seem possible that this could be true. There must be something wrong. Magda had never been given anything quite so generous before and here was Miles, her mentor, giving her a chance to change her world.

'We'll get a passport for you, Magda and then you'll have your new life. Take it.'

'Why would you do this for me, Miles?'

'Because you're worth it, my dear Now dry your eyes and let's get you a drink to celebrate. Janet has already got her bags packed ready to go.'

There didn't seem to be any way that the lonely Magda Kawinski could possibly refuse such a generous offer.

****

Magda was to spend five years in Amarillo, Texas. There, she inhabited a different world from the one she had left behind. In this place of shadows she was, in the beginning, an innocent. But after a while the lies she told and the ones she heard from others became second nature to her. She was able to justify in her own mind what she was doing. She learned not to trust anyone and to treat

157

everyone she met with caution. This was her survival strategy. It worked until one day, she received the summons to return home but to return home, not as Magda Kawinski but as Louisa Ridgeway, for a different identity had been made for her. She held in her hand a new passport with a birth certificate to prove it. The Polish Madga Kawinski no longer existed in the world. Instead there was a Louisa Ridgeway with an English father and a Canadian mother. She set her lips hard and changed her world once more.

****

And now after all those years of being the rather boring Louisa Ridgeway, housewife and mother of two, here was Miles Campbell, holding her hand and telling her once again what he wanted from her.

'There's a man I want you to meet,' he was saying.

'I can't do this anymore, Miles.'

'Ah, but you can, Magda. You and I are alike. We do as we are instructed.'

'I'm not like you, Miles. Never was.'

Miles took her hand and held it tight. He held her hand so tight in his that she felt the pain.

'Remember Josh?' he said. 'One word from me and your comfortable life in the suburbs will be over.'

'Are you threatening me?'

'No, of course not,' he purred. 'But you know what I say is true.'

'There is no truth anymore.'

'You have become a cynic, my dear Magda but whatever else, there is no way out for you. As I said, there is a man I want you to meet and a job to be done.'

A man and a woman passed by the bench. They looked at them as if that was their bench, and Miles and she had no right to be sitting there. Puddles growled. Louisa took hold of his collar. She wished she could get up and walk with the man and the woman, and chat about the weather and the flowers in the park. It would have been easier than having to sit beside Miles and listen to what he was saying but she knew there was no way out, not then, not now.

'What do you want me to do, Miles?' she asked at last.

'Now that's what I wanted to hear,' he said and he pressed a small phial into her hand.

'We don't use pills anymore, Magda. This is more efficient.'

****

Louisa took a sip of sugary tea and looked at her husband. He was studying his mobile phone. He had large stonemason's hands, but those hands could be surprisingly gentle. This was certainly the case when he tapped away on his phone.

'Hey, Lulu,' he said and looked up. Lulu was his pet name for his wife. 'Just read here that Miles Campbell is dead. You know, the union man.'

Louisa did not move a muscle but took another sip of tea.

'Says he collapsed in the street outside Domingo's. Seems he was a regular there. Often thought he didn't have the workers wellbeing at heart, too flashy. Been busy lining his own pocket, if you ask me. Anyone who could afford to dine at Domingo's... well, you know. The likes of you and me wouldn't be allowed through the door, now would we? That place would charge you to breathe!' He chuckled.

'Seems that he was last seen with an Asian man and a dark-haired woman about forty. They were dining with him at Domingo's. How the other live, hey?'

Louisa smiled.

'How indeed?' she murmured.

THE VISIT
A Father Vic Story

Father Vic looked out his window and saw the cold Atlantic waves crashing onto the sand, sweeping back and forth, rolling in and out again. Wind and rain worked together to further bend the black trees at the roadside. Those trees that stayed contoured for all time in their twisted, peculiar shapes, a remembrance of winter's fury. Above black clouds raced across the sky – it was a wild, wild day.

A knock at the door startled him and in came Mrs Ryan, his housekeeper, stout, dependable and sexless – no temptation there – she cooked his meals and tidied his house and left him to return to a husband who was never at home.

'Father Vic,' she was, at times subservient, as if to be obsequious to a priest meant salvation in the afterlife, 'Father Vic, there's a young girl to see you.'

And Father Vic sighed because it wasn't the wild west coast of Ireland outside his window, but the flat, never ending sameness of the Queensland outback and the sky was vibrant blue, not black, and there was no ocean, not for three hundred miles east with a mountain range in the way. It wasn't the Atlantic but the Pacific, and it was the Pacific that had given him his nickname.

Twenty-five years ago, Father Vic had come to this parish, young and eager and straight from Ireland. His name was Oisin, and the first thing that happened to him was that the schoolchildren renamed him. Never having heard that wonderful Celtic name of the legendary warrior, they decided amongst themselves that Oisin sounded like 'ocean', and the only ocean they knew was the 'Pacific'. The sound 'Vic' came at the end of 'Pacific', so Father Vic he became. After a while, he even began to think of himself as 'Vic' and occasionally even wrote 'Vic' instead of 'Oisin' in letters home. He was always amused at the ingenuity of the young; anyway, he often thought, 'Vic' was easier for the Australian tongue, although goodness knows what his dear, sainted mother would have thought, or his father, who loved the Irish Gaelic.

'Do you want to see this girl?' Mrs Ryan interrupted his thoughts, growing impatient. 'She's Irish.'

'Oh... oh... of course, Mrs Ryan... send her in.'

And Father Vic began to shuffle papers on his desk in a distracted fashion not knowing quite what to expect.

A few moments later a bubbly, cheerful young girl of about nineteen bounded into his study, hand outstretched in greeting.

'Hi, Father Vic,' she spoke in a Dublin accent, an educated Dublin accent, it was music to the priest's ears. 'I'm Louise. Louise O'Reilly. My Uncle Bob has a holiday home in Mayo and knows your brother who gave me your address and told me to look you up. You know Ireland, everyone knows someone in Australia... well... here I am! I'm spending a few weeks with the MacMurrays... I met their daughter, Anne, in Brisbane, sure isn't it a small world?'

And she sat down on the only other chair in the room without being invited and gave a huge smile to Father Vic.

In an effort to assimilate all this information, Father Vic also sat down. His brother, ah, his younger brother, Brendan, parish priest too, his mother's favourite. His mother, with two sons priests, must have gone straight to

Heaven, God rest her soul. Father Vic's mind was all a jumble. The MacMurrays, a nice family, he remembered they did have a daughter, although he could never remember her name – but then Louise was off again.

'Oh, your books… how I love books.' She jumped off the chair and was running her hands over the covers, stroking them, loving them.

'I'm studying English Lit at U.C.D.' And she grinned.

Father Vic loved his books too although most of them had been given to him over the years. An old farmer, well read, had been his companion when the young priest first arrived in the parish. Metaphysics, science, religion, politics, literature, they would talk for hours. But then the old farmer died, and Father Vic had been lonely, so very, very lonely. His flock cared for him in a collective way, he knew that, but not one of them had talked to him the way the old farmer had. So here was this girl, this lively, intelligent girl, studying his books in a way no one had done for years.

He had refused to let Mrs Ryan into his inner sanctum with her cloth and polish, no, he had to have one room, but Mrs Ryan would complain that he read too many books and it was doing something to his mind. She appeared in the room at that point, her curiosity aroused, and enquired whether Father and his guest would like a cup of tea, by way of excuse to see what was going on?

Oh, women and their infernal cups of tea, thought Father Vic, crossly, but he just said mildly,

'That would be lovely, Mrs Ryan.' And waved his hand to dismiss her.

Louise smiled again. She seemed so totally and utterly at home in the room, it was like a breath of Ireland had entered and been captured in a small space. Precious, precious moments, Father Vic wanted to hold the moment. The tea came in and was drunk, an hour passed, they hadn't even noticed.

'I'll be off now, Father Vic,' Mrs Ryan came back, suspicious now but knowing her place. 'Your tea's in the oven.'

'Thank you, Mrs Ryan,' said Father Vic, hardly hearing or seeing her presence, because Louise was so enchanting and young and alive. Her mind as sharp as a razor, honed with wisdom well beyond her years.

Another hour passed, and then another. Suddenly, Louise jumped off the chair exclaiming,

'Goodness me, is that the time? I must go.'

And Father Vic desperately, desperately wanted her to stay.

'I'll see you at Mass, then,' he said, hopeful, ever so hopeful. But she just shrugged and seeing this, Father Vic felt a surge of anger. *They have no respect anymore, none whatsoever.*

And then Louise did a surprising thing. She came over to him and held out her arms and held him close. He could feel her soft body, could feel her heart beating. His arms froze at his side, unable to move them. They seemed to be made of blocks of iron and then something happened in his body, he moved and clasped his arms around her shoulders, his head close to hers; the moment remained — it seemed like an eternal moment. And then Louise moved, looked deep into his eyes, he saw her soul, he was sure he saw her soul, and then she smiled, the most beautiful, open, wonderful smile, and she whispered:

'Bless you, Father.'

And left him standing in the middle of the room, motionless, confused and wondering.

WHEN MISS HATCHETT MET SIR GILES

When Miss Hatchett was twenty years of age she danced every dance with Sir Giles at the Hunt Ball. Only he wasn't Sir Giles then, just plain Giles Fortescue-Smythe. What a handsome man he was, with his trimmed black hair, and the Clark Gable moustache. He held her so close that night, she thought she would faint.

Into every life there are pockets of secrecy. Could these hidden secrets await a possible future judgement, of which we do not know, and dare not guess?

In Miss Hatchett's mind, the night of the Hunt Ball was a delicious mixture of youth and optimism and hope. Yes, definitely hope, because hadn't Sir Giles almost proposed marriage to her that night? Miss Hatchett's life changed then. She felt like a woman, and no longer a girl. Sixty long years after, and the indomitable Miss Hatchett hardly ever allowed the past to intrude into the present. But there were just *these* moments. They popped into her mind without any warning. Always these intruders unsettled her, and sometimes they were difficult to send away. What nonsense, she thought, and she looked at herself in the mirror. There was a woman standing there, not too severe, white hair, and a face with lines, not shadows.

Miss Hatchett wove a black silk scarf around her neck. It was going to be cold outside and the frost would stay on the ground. She would be grateful for the warmth of her scarf. Perhaps a small glass of sherry might sustain?

She called to Mrs Lawrence who was busy somewhere, or at least keeping out of the way. That was typical of her housekeeper. On occasions such as this, Mrs Lawrence was difficult to locate, but today she appeared as if by magic, and stood at the doorway, holding a wet cloth in her hand.

'Are you feeling alright, Miss Hatchett?' the housekeeper asked. She thought her employer looked somewhat pale.

'Yes, of course. Could you pour me a sherry, Mrs Lawrence?' said Miss Hatchett and, as an afterthought, she added. 'Just to help me get through today.'

Mrs Lawrence smiled. She was used to the benefits of sherry being expounded in this house, and also its abuses, but Miss Hatchett didn't fall into either category. Although Mrs Lawrence thought Miss Hatchett did take a few drinks on the quiet, so to speak, when no one was around. She filled the sherry glass and handed it to her employer who took a rather large gulp, then sank into the worn tapestry Regency chair beside the pianoforte.

'You know, Mrs Lawrence,' Miss Hatchett said. 'Sir Giles didn't turn out as he started.'

'How's that, then?'

Mrs Lawrence had always found Sir Giles a bore, and he had to be the most dreadful snob imaginable. He was an arrogant fool, full of his own self-importance. A lecherous old fart, too. And Mrs Lawrence sniffed. How could she ever forget that cold December night when Sir Giles, stinking of cigars and whisky, pressed his fat body against hers and tried, and failed, to plant a slobbery kiss onto her lips? She kept out of his way for weeks after that.

'He was very handsome in his youth,' said Miss Hatchett, and she had that distant look on her face that Mrs Lawrence knew only too well.

'I daresay,' replied a sarcastic Mrs Lawrence.

For once Miss Hatchett didn't seem to notice her housekeeper's tone, so preoccupied she was with her own imaginings.

The two women were used to each other. It was a comfortable arrangement, as long as Mrs Lawrence remembered her place, for Miss Hatchett never forgot hers. Miss Hatchett almost, just almost, was about to enquire whether her housekeeper would like to share a sherry with her as it seemed perhaps, appropriate for the occasion, and could do no harm? But before she could say anything, her sister, Elizabeth, came bounding into the room. Neither Miss Hatchett nor Mrs Lawrence had heard her enter the house. Elizabeth was younger than Miss Hatchett by five years, and a good four inches shorter. Like her sister, she was thin and tweedy, with long legs and long arms. Elizabeth's fingers were always adorned with rings; diamonds and precious stones, being her favourites. She never left the house without applying a vibrant red polish onto her manicured nails. Elizabeth had a great liking for gold bracelets, too, and had started wearing even more of them. With all her jewellery, Miss Hatchett often thought, and said, on more than one occasion, that her sister clanked too much! Today, however, Elizabeth was dressed in black.

'It's perishing out there,' she said in a loud voice and, without waiting for an answer, she took hold of the bottle of sherry. With one magnificent gulp, Elizabeth downed a glassful, and then without uttering another word, refilled her glass, right to the top. Mrs Lawrence hovered, uncertain as to what was expected of her.

'Well, let's get it over and done with,' Elizabeth boomed. 'Giles would not want to be kept waiting.'

'Your tardiness did exasperate him, and you never took a blind bit of notice, did you, dear?' answered Miss Hatchett, and a mischievous smile appeared.

'Oh, well... I won't be late for his funeral. That should please him,' said Elizabeth, airily.

Mrs Lawrence withdrew with the empty glasses, leaving the bottle of sherry, a quarter full now, on the drinks table.

'Come on then, old thing,' said Elizabeth. 'Mustn't keep the old boy waiting!'

'Are you going to be a merry widow now, dear?' asked Miss Hatchett, hooking her arm through her sister's and, with just a flicker of amusement in her blue eyes, those same eyes that had captivated Sir Giles all those years ago on that one night, and only that night.

'You just watch me,' laughed her sister.

'I certainly will, Elizabeth, my dear.'

Miss Hatchett's thoughts were full of hope now. Could the memories, once and for all, be laid to rest beside Sir Giles, along with her youth, and what might have been?

THE OISIN KELLY SERIES

CRYING THROUGH THE WIND

This is the tale of Oisin Kelly, beginning with his mother, Annie as she struggles to come to terms with her love for two brothers in a small West of Ireland community in the 1950's.

Married to Bernard, she is attracted to his brother, the mysterious and much misunderstood Mick. Annie's strong Catholic faith engenders a deep sense of guilt, at the same time it helps her to cope.

The story moves forwards, sometimes gently, sometimes turbulently all the time combining pathos with humour. Although *Crying Through the Wind* is very much Annie's book, the stage is set for Oisin who has a quest of his own. First published 2014, 2nd edition 2018.
ISBN: 978-1-909411-30-2

FAMILIAR YET FAR

Young Irishman, Oisin Kelly, bitter and disillusioned leaves Britain vowing never to return. When he arrives in the outback Australian town of Kilgoolga his life is still haunted by past events. Struggling to come to terms with his new and sometimes frightening environment, he falls under the spell of the enigmatic Eleanor Bradshaw. Deception, intrigue and misplaced loyalty are at the heart of this work of fiction as Oisin discovers that things are not always what they seem. First published 2015. 2nd edition 2018.
ISBN: 978-1-909411-39-5

HOMECOMING

Oisin Kelly has put down roots in the outback Queensland town of Kilgoolga. Here his life becomes entwined with Vietnam War veteran, Harry. Past traumatic events affect both men in similar and sometimes surprising ways. As

Oisin discovers more and more hidden secrets, he begins
to wonder where his life is leading, and where his true
home really is. Decisions have to be made as to which force
is more powerful. Will it be the power of love over evil that
will triumph and bring him home? Published 2018.
ISBN: 978-1-912513-82-6

THE CANDLE BURNS LOW
Oisin's story continues...

Silver Quill Publishing

Silver Quill is an exciting new publishing group producing fabulous books for children teens, young – and not so young – adults. Take a look at our website, meet our authors and browse through the titles we have to offer. Every book is a thrill with Silver Quill.

www.silverquillpublishing.com

www.ingramcontent.com/pod-product-compliance
Lightning Source LLC
Chambersburg PA
CBHW030632190726
48286CB00008B/2499